RED RIVER STAGE

Western Stories

RED RIVER STAGE

Western Stories

Fred Grove

Five Star • Waterville, Maine

An earlier version of the Foreword by Johnny D. Boggs
appeared in *Tucson Lifestyle* (11/00).

Five Star First Edition Western Series.

Published in 2001 in conjunction with
Golden West Literary Agency.

Set in 11 pt. Plantin by Rick Gundberg.

Printed in the United States on permanent paper.

Library of Congress Cataloging-in-Publication Data

Grove, Fred.
    Red River stage : western stories / by Fred Grove. — 1st ed.
        p.   cm.
    "Five Star western."
    Contents: When the caballos came — The marshal of
Indian Rock — Comanche woman — Face of danger — Be
brave, my son — The town killer — The homeseekers —
Mystery of the mountain light — A day in the forest —
Beyond the ridge — Gunfighter's choice — Red River stage.
    ISBN 0-7862-3262-5 (hc : alk. paper) 2465 2161
    1. Western stories. I. Title.
PS3557.R7 R43 2001
    813'.54—dc21   2001023676

DEDICATION
To Jon Tuska, a Westerner

Table of Contents

Foreword
by Johnny D. Boggs

Fred Grove can trace the beginnings of his writing career to a night in 1923 when he was just a boy in Fairfax, Oklahoma. Grove, his mother, and uncle were home when they heard a tremendous explosion. "The next morning we found that an Osage Indian's house had been blown up with nitroglycerin," the novelist recalled. "That made a rather lasting impression."

Grove, who is of Osage and Sioux descent, chronicled those cruel Osage murders of the 1920s in two novels, WARRIOR ROAD (Doubleday, 1974) and DRUMS WITHOUT WARRIORS (Doubleday, 1976). He has also written about the War Between the States and quarter horse racing in the Southwest. Mostly, however, he writes about the post-Civil War American frontier—cowboy stories . . . shoot-em-ups . . . oaters . . . Westerns. And he has been pretty successful at it.

"Fred Grove's Indian heritage gives him unique insight when he writes about Native Americans and his love for and knowledge of horses has given many of his novels a unique slant," Western novelist Elmer Kelton has said of Grove. "In addition to his specialized knowledge, he is a dickens of a good writer, so Fred Grove stories have always offered something special."

Grove has won five Spur Awards—the Pulitzer for Western writers—from the Western Writers of America. His

9

two Spur award-winning short stories—"Comanche Woman" (1963) and "When the *Caballos* Came" (1968)—are collected together here for the first time. Grove also has been honored with two Western Heritage Awards from the National Cowboy Hall of Fame, a Levi Strauss Golden Saddleman Award from the WWA, an Oklahoma Writing Award from the University of Oklahoma and, for his fiction about the Apache frontier, a Distinguished Service Award from Western New Mexico University.

"I never got rich at writing, monetarily," Grove admitted, who moved with his wife Lucile to Tucson after nineteen years in New Mexico to be closer to their son, William. "But to me the Western story is the American story, a continuing thing that started way back East."

Nor did he get rich working on newspaper before, during, and after World War II. "The most I ever made was sixty-five dollars a week, and, when I got up there, I thought I was snapping that up," explained Grove.

Writing about the West came naturally to Grove. His mother was born on the Sioux reservation in Pine Ridge, South Dakota, and his father, as a teenager, rode on several trail drives from Texas to the northern pastures. One of the writer's professors at the University of Oklahoma was the great Western historian Walter Campbell, who wrote under the name Stanley Vestal and once introduced Grove to Texas folklorist J. Frank Dobie. Another teacher told him: "You're closer to the frontier than you realize." After graduating from OU in 1937 and beginning a newspaper career, Grove uncovered the truth of the statement.

"Working on newspapers, particularly in Shawnee, Oklahoma, I interviewed a lot of Oklahoma pioneers, people who had made land runs, and that got me going again on writing Westerns." One thing led to another, finally settling in Tucson and writing about the Apache frontier.

Grove started writing novels for Ballantine Books. He tended to write series. In addition to the two novels about the Osage murders, he has written a series of horse stories that includes the two Spur winners THE GREAT HORSE RACE (Doubleday, 1977) and MATCH RACE (Doubleday, 1982). In the series, horse trader Dude McQuinn, owning one fast horse, and sidekicks Coyote Walking and Uncle Billy Lockhart, "would go down to a saloon and tell a few lies and race the local champion, clean up, and get out of town." He wrote a couple of novels about the slaughter of the buffalo, and four books, so far, the most recent being his Tucson-set INTO THE FAR MOUNTAINS (Five Star Westerns, 1999), about Jesse Wilder, a former Confederate officer ostracized by his family after joining the Union Army to fight on the frontier rather than die in a prison camp.

"He's just been doing it forever," said his wife Lucile. "We got married in Nineteen Thirty-Eight, he started writing then, and he's been doing it ever since. He takes a lot of facts and works them in. He has studied the territory and doesn't put anything down unless he thinks it's right. Writing's a lonely life, but I don't mind. I've enjoyed it."

Grove is pleased with his career, and doesn't listen to naysayers who predict the death of the Western novel. "The West is so big and vast," he said. "There's so much to write about there. I think right now it seems like the Western story's doing pretty well."

And so is Fred Grove, the 88-year-old novelist.

Johnny D. Boggs

When the *Caballos* Came

Grayfoot picked his way up the stony face of the bald ridge, his leg muscles twitching from the long climb. At the top, swaying in weariness, he could feel the parched breath of the southwest wind as he looked out upon the shimmering plain below, speckled with reddish dust, glazed with burning sun.

Nothing moved. Under the shivering heat waves the land seemed to be drifting and twisting, unreal to the eye. Far out, something flashed. Again he saw it. Not one but several sun flashes. And now a low mass crawling snake-like over the plain, moving northeast, and he thought of the buffalo he must find for his hungry camp.

At once he went long striding down the slope. The flashes puzzled him. But he knew that when the great sun hung straight overhead, as it did now, it caused everything between earth and sky to glitter and dance, and all objects looked strange.

On the plain he struck a tireless trot, the rawhide soles of his moccasins husking through the short grass, a sinew-wrapped, wooden-handled flint knife swinging at his belt. Presently the blowing wind dropped to a soft whimper, and across the blue arch of the clearing sky landmarks seemed to stalk toward him: a broken butte, a humped ridge.

He saw the flickering flashes again, and a sensation akin to fear brushed him. But now he could see a broad column, its figures dim in the haze of dust they stirred. But not a dark mass like buffalo. It was strange.

Curious, he trotted to a grass-trimmed rise and crouched down to watch. Little by little the dusty column grew more distinct. He saw walking figures, carrying what looked like long sticks or lances. Behind them. . . .

He gave a start, his gaze stabbing on a blur of white. Behind them he saw the strangest sight of his young life. A man riding a four-footed animal as white as snow. Something that shone covered much of the rider's body. The sun flashed on it, and Grayfoot knew it was such brightness he had spied from the ridge. It was all strange.

He shrank flat down, watching the hazy figures advance. Now he caught the hum of men's voices, the tramping of feet, and sharp clatterings and clankings, and a menacing sound like nothing he had heard before: the *clopping* the four-footed creature made as his sharp feet trampled the earth.

He stared, both awed and apprehensive. The creature was powerful and proud and stood higher than a warrior's head. A glossy mane hung over the arching neck. The long white tail, carried high, almost brushed the curly grass.

Looking beyond, Grayfoot saw coming many other animals the size of the white one. Solid colors. More whites. A few blacks. Some grays. Some dark red ones. Some bright red ones.

The sight flung a quickening excitement through him. Could these be the swift-running creatures that his people, the Penateka Comanches, had heard about from wanderers of tribes to the west? The terrible creatures the white eyes had brought?

As the first rider was passing, his body shining, a tuft of feathers slanting from the shiny object protecting his head, Grayfoot saw the brown hair covering his angular face, the pale skin on his forehead. He carried his head high, as proud as the prancing beast he rode. He guided it with long leather reins extending from its jaws. He sat on a broad pad of leather, shaped high behind with a horn in front.

In advance walked two white eyes shouldering shiny sticks. Between them strode an Indian, naked to the waist, his black hair chopped short, and a leather band around his head. Grayfoot recognized him as from the Tejas living far to the west. It was he who led the way.

Now the trampling became a steady drumming, and the dust thickened as more four-footed animals began passing, their skins sleek and smooth in the brilliant sun. He admired each one, yet was glad that he was no nearer the sharp feet. The red creatures held his attention the longest. Next he saw burdened Indian slaves, other Tejas, leading spare animals and some with packs. How much greater burdens they carried on their backs, he thought, than the dogs in his camp pulling the light poles on which his people lashed their belongings.

As the last Tejas straggled by, he raised up to look. His eyes clung to the strange animals, lingering on the red-skinned ones, their proud heads nodding as they drew away. As powerful and fierce as they looked, they were the most beautiful living things he had ever seen.

He continued to watch them, his eyes glowing. Then, with a feeling of mixed fear and fascination, he trotted after them.

Throughout the afternoon he trailed the dusty procession, sometimes in its wake, sometimes on either flank, or watching from a stand of mesquites or from behind an outcrop of rocks, always out of sight, content just to observe the creatures and their habits. When the column rested at a stream, he saw the beasts nibble the short grass like the buffalo and drink like the buffalo, and he was pleased. Never did the cringing Tejas ride the spare creatures, and, although the Tejas led them and saw to the packs, he noticed their fear.

Before dusk the white eyes camped below a high, yellow bluff, where a spring gushed and formed a wide pool. Grayfoot, spellbound, watched while the Tejas led the animals to water and afterward took them out on the prairie and drove stakes into the ground and tied them with ropes so they could graze like the buffalo.

Darkness purpled the cooling land when he slipped to the pool and drank. There he ate sparingly from his scant supply of dried buffalo meat. Beyond him rose high-pointed tents, as pale in the half light as the faces of the white eyes, and the torches throwing flickering images on the tent walls, and the humble Tejas slinking fearfully about.

He could hear the four-footed ones snuffling and stamping their feet while they grazed. The wind lifted, and he pointed his nose upward like a wolf and sniffed their strange, sweaty scent, liking its keenness. Stirred, he felt himself drawn toward them.

At that moment he saw a figure, and he melted deeper into the bluff's shadows. The man came ahead, and Grayfoot stopped, seeing that it was an Indian. A low voice asked: "Who are you?"

Grayfoot told him.

"A Penateka? Why do you follow us?"

"It's the four-footed ones," Grayfoot explained, excitement rising in his voice. "What strange creature is this?"

The Indian looked fearfully about him. His voice became hushed. "The white eyes call it the *caballo* . . . the horse."

"The horse?"

"True. But to us, the Tejas, it is the Big Dog. Did you notice the heavy packs?"

"I saw," Grayfoot said. "Why don't you ride the spare *caballos?*"

The dim figure shuddered. "We are afraid. The white eyes tell us these creatures are monsters that, when angered, will devour us."

A coldness passed over Grayfoot. "Have you seen them do this dreadful thing?"

"No . . . but it is true."

"Yet today I saw them eat grass and drink water like the buffalo."

"You are too young to understand these strange things." He turned to go. "Don't follow us. This is a bad camp. Everyone is afraid."

He slept that night in a mesquite thicket and dreamed that he rode one of the terrible monsters a great distance, so swiftly that the land blurred before his eyes and the wind tore at his face; and that he had won a new name because of his deed, and his old nickname, given to him as a small boy when he had danced in the dead ashes of a campfire, and which he did not like, was rubbed out. Of a sudden, before he could learn his new name, the dream vanished like smoke and he awoke, chilled and hungry.

Eating the last strip of his food, he crept closer and watched the camp stir. Seldom did his eyes stray from the *caballos,* so sleek and clean-limbed. How, he asked himself, deeply puzzled, could an animal be beautiful and yet a monster? Still, the Tejas' fear was real.

At last, the vast camp came together and formed a loose line and began traveling northwest.

He hung back. Even though he returned to his hungry camp without sighting buffalo, he would be welcomed and given food. If he followed the monster horses, he would go hungry, and they might eat him, if he got too close.

He stood like stone. As the column rose over a grassy swell, the rays of the morning sun struck the glossy hide of a red horse, shimmering on it until the animal seemed bathed in fire.

He delayed no longer. A wonderful excitement sent him trotting. When the sun stood highest over the red earth, he saw the white eyes rest themselves near a creek while the cowering Tejas made cooking fires; others gingerly led the horses to water and grazed them. He could feel only pity for such slaves, for the most important thing in a Penateka's life was to be brave and generous and faithful to his people. And by now he knew he would follow the beautiful *caballos* as long as breath stayed in his body, until he knew whether they were friend or monster.

Hunger gnawed at him. He forced it from his mind, because times of want were frequent among the foot-bound Penatekas, and often he practiced self-denial. He busied himself studying the grazing shapes, their graceful necks, their long manes whipping softly in the wind.

A tiny rustling reached him. He turned and saw a flat, roundish creature waddling through the grass, yellow spots and bars on its shelled back. He captured the terrapin and cooked it over one of the buffalo chip fires the white eyes had left smoldering. Gorging on the rich meat, he felt strength flow all through him. He drank at the creek and followed on.

He caught up with the column as it was angling across a shallow valley below him. Ahead of the white eyes the earth was black with buffalo, so many they blocked the way. This was the season when the frisky calves born in the green of spring still had their reddish coats, and when, he knew, their watchful mothers and the bulls guarded them fiercely.

Now some of the white eyes rode out and pointed the long sticks at the buffalo. Grayfoot saw smoke puffs and heard the following loud *bangs*. He saw the buffalo begin to stir. A ripple ran through the herd. The valley seemed to be moving. In moments he saw the entire mass lurch into motion. A rumbling roar rose.

Too late, he saw the lead white eyes turn their horses to race out of danger. He flinched as if from a blow as the leading wedge of the buffalo struck the first riders and rolled on to smash into the milling column. Horses broke loose. Tejas were scurrying like rabbits.

Out of the boiling dust rushed a red horse trailing long reins. After it ran a white eyes in fruitless pursuit. He ran a way and stopped, watching the horse flee back down the trail.

The horse swept up the slope toward Grayfoot, who froze as he waited for the monster to charge him. Instead, it wheeled aside, a wildness bulging the fiery eyes. In that flashing moment he saw that the horse was as red as the great sun, and a white blaze dripped the length of the proud face to the wide-flaring nostrils.

For a breath he could not act, he could only stare. Another moment and he was following the horse before he quite realized he was, fearfully, also, as if fate pointed him that way.

Steadily the red horse ran along the gouged trail. It took all Grayfoot's endurance to stay in sight. He trotted across a wide plain toward a huddle of knobby hills. There the horse disappeared. But when Grayfoot strained to the first rise, he discovered the horse halted on the trail, head flung high, alert.

A feeling opened in Grayfoot, a new awareness—he must see the horse up close, dangerous as that might be. He moved on the impulse, to circle in from the flank. He was close enough to see the muscles rippling under the sun-red hide when the horse uttered a whistling snort and bounded off the trail. It had, Grayfoot knew, caught his scent.

As the sun tilted downward into the quivering heat of afternoon, Grayfoot's doubts rose, and, dream-like, he wondered why his new name eluded him. Was it because he had failed to finish his deed? A vague and deeper sense drove him on. He must be brave. He must even touch the monster horse. Yes. A cold fear slid over him, and he thought of his people far away.

His strength lessened as the day wore on, as he saw that the horse was beginning to circle. If he cut across the circle each time, could he walk the horse down?

It became almost a game: the horse traveling in shorter circles, Grayfoot trotting grimly across. He moved through a kind of tortured haze, relieved only when he spied the flash of the strange animal he pursued, perhaps to his own death.

He stumbled to the crown of a rocky ridge and saw the horse grazing below. Beyond rolled broken country, mesquite thickets, wicked draws, and brushy cañons that, he saw, dead-ended against the eroded wall rimming the basin. Why had the horse come here? He saw the answer in the glint of a spring-fed branch. The horse had smelled water.

He began working along the ridge, so that, when he started across, the wind would be from the horse toward him. His only chance was to drive the horse into one of the cañons, then touch the monster when he ran out.

Down now, the wind to him, he was fairly close before the horse took alarm and wheeled for open country. Grayfoot, darting right, waved the red one back. Galloping, it cut for the cañon where the water was, Grayfoot running after. Just as the cañon walls closed around him, he saw the horse, boxed in, whirl to break out. Again Grayfoot waved his arms; again the horse gave ground.

Instinct told Grayfoot not to crowd in. He had but to touch the red monster to perform his brave deed. But as he approached, the horse, like a flash, leaped the branch and raced down the cañon to Grayfoot's left, leather reins dragging.

He drew back in fear—then a desperation flung him across the little stream and diving for the reins. He missed, he clutched, he felt the stout leather hissing through his hands. He tightened his grip and felt himself dragged over gravel, now grass, with the sharp feet thundering in his ears, his punished body burning. Mesquites blurred ahead. When the horse hesitated before a thicket, Grayfoot tried to scramble to his feet. The horse cut away, and Grayfoot was jerked rolling against a spiny trunk. The horse swung violently around, snared fast by the reins tangled in the thicket and whose ends Grayfoot still gripped.

He lay there some moments, too winded and punished to rise. He staggered up, his raw body slick with blood and dirt. He gazed at his captive. At the blazed face, the broad forehead, the pointed fox ears, the black mane and tail, the small muzzle, the soft, luminous eyes, in them an expression that somehow made Grayfoot feel guilt. The red horse dripped sweat, and his sides were heaving. His strong smell flowed to Grayfoot, strange, yet pleasing.

A feeling swelled in Grayfoot. "Horse," he said, "I am not afraid of you," although his trembling voice betrayed him. "If you are brave, why did you run from the buffalo? Speak to me!" The horse said no word and blew through his delicate nostrils, which perhaps was his strange talk, and Grayfoot said, haltingly: "I . . . I am going to touch you."

His movement around the thicket straightened the reins, and the backing-up horse pulled them free. Eyes wild, it reared up powerfully. Grayfoot, jerked down, tensed for the first pouncing bite. But he felt nothing. The horse was struggling to pull free.

"Horse," he said, up quickly, "are you not hungry?"

Still, his fear stayed. Taking up on the reins, he lifted his hand, hesitated, then touched the quivering muzzle. It felt softer than buckskin in that one instant before the tossing head shook off his hand.

His brain reeling in exultation, he stepped back. His deed was performed. He could let the horse go now. Yet he did not. Moments slipped by. He kept admiring the horse, while a curious longing for possession stole over him.

"Horse," he said, "listen to me. I have done my deed. Now we can be friends. I will ride as the white eyes ride."

In his eagerness, he drew the reins around the arched neck as he had watched the white eyes do, and rushed to mount from the left side. The horse sprang away, and Grayfoot stumbled. He rushed in again; once more the horse shied away. Looking into the wild eyes, he realized that the animal was as frightened of him as he had been of it in the beginning.

Shortening up on the reins, he caressed the blazed nose, the broad forehead, the pointed ears, and breathed into the quivering nostrils so that the horse could smell him.

He was ready to try again when a late thought passed through his mind. The white eyes had mounted him from the right side, not the left.

Slower this time, he eased to the right side, conscious that the horse was trembling. Grayfoot drew a deep breath, reached for the high horn, and swung to the leather seat, crouched for trouble.

The horse seemed to wait. Uncertain what to do, Grayfoot lifted the reins. To his immense astonishment and joy, the red horse moved off at a slow walk, now a hard trot, now a soft gallop, and, as it swept into a stretching run, Grayfoot seemed borne upward on the exuberant wind and his plains world seemed to open up for him as if he saw it for the first time.

As swiftly he knew his new name. It was He Brings the Horse.

The Marshal of Indian Rock

A smoky dust was still hanging in the dry air when Buck Dancy stepped down from the Indian Rock stage. A high man, slack-shouldered and long of arm, he turned to watch the other passengers gather up their belongings. Afterward, he claimed his own leather grip and moved up the street, feeling a familiar depression already settling. He moved toward the row of high-faced frame buildings, his attention at once on the fair-skinned man waiting in the shade of Hoffman's Saddle Shop. The usual reception, Buck decided, as the man stepped forward, eyes sharpening.

"I guess you're Dancy," he said, staring.

Buck, nodding, took the outstretched hand, soft as a woman's and quickly withdrawn.

"I'm Arthur Crowder." The tone was direct, and Buck remembered the urgent letter. "I got in touch with you for the Citizens' Committee." Crowder's voice bordered on impatience with a tinge of self-importance that Buck did not miss. "There was considerable hurry because we're short a town marshal. Old Mike Haney's in Pawnee with three bullets in him. Peace officers don't last long here." Crowder raised his square-on glance again.

Unimpressed, Buck felt himself scowling as he met the long look, aware of his rising annoyance at being set apart and gawked at. He forced it back wearily, through controlled habit. "What did you expect?" he said with thin amusement. "Some wild man with four Colts and a Bowie knife to cut notches?"

Color climbed into Crowder's face. "I guess," he said, giving a hasty, pushed-out laugh, "it's because you don't look like a notori . . . I mean a famous peace officer. I was expecting a hardcase, and older."

"I know." Buck shrugged, and the ancient fatigue came on him and a resentment of Crowder's slip. Because notorious *was* what he'd meant. You soon acquired a reputation, if you survived this solitary game, and you were expected to look the awesome part. You took the stares, always more curious than friendly, although you never got used to them.

Slowly Buck let his temper die, and he eyed Crowder, appraising him. He was a tall man, somehow out of place here on the frontier where the new land rolled up to the broad river, an almost handsome blond man with fine features the savage prairie sun would always burn. A man whose moody face showed the pull of unbounded ambition, a kind of rashness.

The man, with a trace of restlessness, said: "This evening you'll meet with the committee. There'll be questions." Buck felt himself measured and sized up again. Then Crowder, half turning in his walk, added: "I picked you for the job," and Buck thought dryly: *You've put your money on a horse you figure's fast enough to win.* Crowder's stare hung on, bright, asking for reassurance.

Contempt rose in Buck, and he ignored the man to read the sign in this territory town, methodically filing the details away. The low-roofed sandstone jail, the gray-weathered string of buildings. The beaten street, the single pulse-beat. Deceptively quiet in daylight, as now with the clump of horses tail-switching flies in front of the Boomer Saloon.

Buck thought of an awakening old renegade, stirring to smoke and noise in the night. If Indian Rock was no Abilene, Oglala, or Caldwell where Charlie Stewart had died doing his job, it was a bad place to have your gun stick.

Below the town he could see the shallow Arkansas, the river sand bleached and shimmering. Timber stood in thick files on the far, green bank, with beyond it the knuckled hills. They raked up a quick hunger, something distant and waiting, a phantom still mocking him through all these years. Always in his mind had been the desire to take up land. He guessed it went back to the rich Missouri soil that he had known before striking out for fabled Texas. Yet he had held off at the thought of trying it alone. In his quieter moments, he knew it was because of the loneliness, the uncertainty. Even as a peace officer you had people around you, friendly or not, and forever drawing you on was the challenge of another wild trail town.

Crowder lifted a hand, long-fingered and white. "That's the Osage country over there across the river. Kent Beeler's country. You'll hear about him soon enough."

They moved up the street, and, as it flattened out, Buck saw the black lettering on a fly-specked office window: **Arthur B. Crowder, Attorney at Law**. Next door, at the Pawnee Hotel, Crowder stopped and said in apology, spreading his soft hands: "Not much, but the food's good."

A dark-haired young woman stood at the door, pieces of dress material over her arm. Her eyes, watching Crowder, held a pleased expression. "Ma Price," she said with mock dismay, "wants a rose pattern. I would be out of that."

"Whatever you have, it will take plenty of it," laughed Crowder, possessively taking her arm. "Hetty, this is Buck Dancy. Miss Ahrens has the distinction of being Indian Rock's only dressmaker."

Buck held his hat and said: "Miss Ahrens, I'm mighty glad to meet you." She wore a bright blue dress, and he noticed the ivory shading of her neck against the ruffles. She had a full, striking face and rather high cheek bones. She regarded him, the gray eyes frank and smiling, until Crowder spoke significantly: "This is Dancy . . . *Buck Dancy* . . . going to be the new marshal."

Her glance slid about in sudden understanding. When she looked at Buck again, curiously, he had the feeling that she was displeased.

"Without the horns," he said, but she didn't smile.

"I've heard of you." Her voice was polite and complete rejection.

In that moment, Buck saw himself. A big-boned man trimmed down too hard and the mark of his chancy trade stamped on him. He was staring after her, watching her go with a flutter of long skirts into a shop close by, when Crowder's voice brought him around. "I'm going to marry that girl."

"You're a lucky man." Buck stepped inside. He signed the register while the clerk looked on. Crowder followed upstairs.

"There's something you should know," he said. "Solomon Wight, who owns the Boomer, figures this town should suit the saloon trade. He's thick with Beeler."

Buck took this in, feeling surprise without showing it. "I'll remember that."

"Eight o'clock, remember, over Tarpley's store."

For some while Buck thought of the tall, cool girl and of Arthur Crowder, whose wildness lay printed in pale tracks across his high-strung face. Coming out of the dining room after supper, he saw a heavy-bodied woman behind the desk.

"Never thought I'd have the real Buck Dancy in *my* place," she greeted him, brassy and friendly. "I'm Ma Price.

Welcome to Injun Rock. You've seen worse and you'll see better." She studied him, judging him, approving him. "No secret why *you're* here."

"Business." He canted his head at the still street, listening.

"Quiet now," she told him. "Wolves don't howl till the church folks . . . what few there are . . . go to bed. If there's ever a mass hangin', we'll have to send to Kansas City for rope."

Her laugh rolled out, and he smiled and went outside, suddenly sober. Checking himself, testing the current of the street down which early riders drifted in, he could feel wind lifting off the prairie, grass sweet and cool. He drew the fragrance in deeply before his restlessness, coming on, drove him forward. He ended his swing on the far side in front of Tarpley's Mercantile, short of the blazing Boomer Saloon. There were other whisky mills, but the Boomer was king. He heard a woman's tired voice and the off-key thump of an ancient piano.

He watched and smoked, the cigar dull and flat. At eight he climbed the stairs over the store. Four men sat around a table with Arthur Crowder, and Buck sensed they had been there a good while. It was Crowder who rose and spoke their names. Buck shook hands with Solomon Wight and Adam Tarpley, with Hap Spann, who ran the Pioneer Livery, and Mack Rains. Buck read Rains at a glance, a surly, thick-chested watchdog at Wight's elbow. His light-colored eyes showed sly interest while he chewed on a match stem.

Still standing, Buck regarded them with a feeling that brushed indifference. Years ago he'd have jumped at the chance to take on a new town for five hundred dollars a month. Now he said flatly: "There are certain matters about this job I want made clear." He saw Wight's head come up. "A peace officer can't keep order playing a skimmed-milk game. He can't keep it with blood in his eye. Neither can he work with interference, aimed at improving business for one side of the street."

Wight stared at the tip of his black cigar. "Indian Rock," he said, "is no ordinary town, Mister Dancy. We all know Kent Beeler's boys are wild. Most of them have records in the States. But a part of our trade comes from across the river, whether we like it or not. We get only a fair play on this side from the ranchers and settlers. Lean too far either way and we lose. Mike Haney played it too rough. No understanding of business problems. I say let the boys have their fun."

Buck gave Wight a closer attention. Not a big man, he looked big. His shoulders were solid bulges of muscle, his neck a short, powerful column. Shrewd, speculative black eyes looked out on a cynical world in which little escaped him or, Buck guessed, foxed him.

"That's about it," agreed Spann, an easy-going smooth face.

All at once, Tarpley shoved back from the table and stood up. "I will put it stronger than that for the other side," he declared, and looked Wight in the eyes. "This Osage bunch is driving decent people away. More cowmen are leasing the Pawnee and Oto grasslands. We could get more homesteaders. They will be here long after Beeler's buried and forgotten." He swiveled his stubborn gaze around. "I want Dancy to crack down. Give us a clean town." He had a Yankee's blunt frankness, an uncompromising distrust for softhanded methods.

There was a run of silence as Tarpley sat down. They waited on Crowder now. Buck watched his lips pinch together, saw caution. "Dancy's the man to handle it," Crowder said, yet, saying it, sounded evasive. "He will be fair."

"I will try to be," Buck said, "but it will have to be done my way. Without interference." He heard his voice forming the usual words, conscious of a weighted weariness. "I've seen some good officers . . . Wild Bill, Tilghman, the Earps, and Charlie Stewart."

"Stewart's dead," Wight said promptly. "Saw it in Caldwell."

"That's right." Buck nodded, holding his voice down. "Shot in the back trying to break up a hanging. He happened to be my best friend." Wight's eyes were unreadable. Buck's voice drove into him. "Troublemakers will get first call. Beeler's crew included. That understood?"

Tarpley's head jerked agreement, but the others, undecided, eyed Wight and waited. He was silent for half a minute, stiff-faced. "All right. But don't ruin this town. Takes more than a Spanish bit to break a wild horse. Remember that."

Wight was the key. The meeting adjourned. Wight let the townsmen flow past him. Buck met his stare. "This is a town with the hair on," Wight said.

"So I hear." For once Buck let his bitterness spill over. "Haney get it in the back, too?"

Wight's face never changed. "Come to think of it, he did. Haney had his enemies." His mouth spread into an easy grin. "Marshals drink on the house at the Boomer," he said, and walked out. Rains threw Buck a narrowed look and followed.

When Buck came down to the street, the woman with the seamy voice was singing again, while the race-horse piano player ran the keys. Riders came yowling from the darkness of the river ford. They swung in at the Boomer, swirling up dust that gritted between Buck's teeth. Sallow light slanting from saloon row made a greasy shine on horseflesh rowed along the hitch racks. A bleak feeling touched him as he observed the flow of traffic into this outlaw town. Beginning his usual slow stroll, he observed a mechanical watchfulness and, threading the planks crowded with booted men, he was alone again, following a familiar path.

For three days he paced the street, and there was an uneasy calm in Indian Rock.

"The longest peace we've ever had," Adam Tarpley informed him. "I believe your reputation has put the fear into these wild men. It is good to see."

Buck shook his head. "They're not afraid of me. We haven't had the right mixture yet. It will come when a Beeler rider and some cowboy get enough tanglefoot at the same time."

Each twilight Buck stood alone in front of the hotel, waiting, showing a patience he didn't really have for the violence that always came. The fourth night he had stationed himself in the early shadows, when a horse pounded in off the Pawnee Trail. The rider swung down and hurried inside. Presently, Hetty Ahrens came along the walk. He could almost time her arrival in the cool of the evening to visit Ma Price. She entered the hotel, nodding, and he lifted his hat. Seeing her again, he realized he looked forward to this break in the lonely routine, to their few brief words before she started home.

Thought slid away on the sound of loud talk. Simultaneously two riders trotted in from the west—ranch hands. As Buck watched them dismount by the Boomer's rack, Hetty Ahrens left the hotel suddenly.

Over his shoulder, Buck said: "Might be a good idea to get inside. Never know what a drunk will do with a gun." It occurred to him then her visit had been short. Feeling her eyes upon him, he swung around, vaguely disturbed. She seemed taller in the half light from the door, shadow-eyed.

"What is it?" Her voice was low, almost detached.

"Party's getting bigger over there." He turned away, hearing the voices again, flat and sharp. He saw her take a step, and hesitate.

"I guess you can feel it. That's why they hired you. We know your story. You started driving cattle. The gun fever got you. You learned to tame towns, became a professional with a name. Men have tried to kill you . . . somebody will. What can you hope to find in this?"

Her words, so close to the truth, spun him back. He had a queer feeling then. "Why," he said, momentarily startled, "I'll quit someday."

"You'll wait too long."

"Indian Rock will cool down. Once the wildness wears off, I'll go somewhere else. There's new land west of here. One of these days. . . ." He broke off, knowing he was clumsy before this cool woman.

"Then why do you wait?" She moved, her shape slim, her large eyes solemn and frank. "There's a man from Pawnee . . . Mike Haney died today."

He started to speak, and it caught up with him, shaking him. Why had she deliberately withheld word of Haney's death until the last?

Voices ground out hard by Wight's saloon. A single shot sounded across the street.

Buck took Hetty's arm. "Get inside," he said.

He saw the knot of men, and, as he stepped toward them, somebody rushed past, yelling: "Tip Steves shot Johnny Garr!"

Buck halted along the rim of scattered light, taking in the groaning cowboy flattened close to the Boomer's doors. His partner stood rigid before a young-faced man who teetered on boot heels, waving a pistol. A big-hatted rider made a move toward the horses. "Tip!" he called. "Come on!"

"No saddle-bum's crowdin' me!" Tip answered.

Buck drew breath to the bottom of his lungs, slipped out his pistol, and stepped behind the horses. When he cut in, he saw Steves, swaying, half faced away from him. Buck said— "Put it up."—and closed in.

Steves wheeled, gun lifting. This was the game that Buck knew well. He swung his gun. He felt the barrel connect, the impact jarring along his arm muscles. Steves, groaning, crashed backward against the saloon wall. Frantic, the man strained to drag up his weapon. Buck sledged him savagely, heard Steves cry out. The fellow grabbed his smashed wrist. His six-shooter clattered on the planks.

It was over. Buck's eyes went to the wounded man, swept across the ranked circle of watchers. "Get a doctor," he ordered wearily.

At last, a man detached himself and went running across the street. There was a pushing out from inside the saloon. Buck, anxious to avoid the crowd, shoved his prisoner into motion. He forced Steves down the street at a rapid walk to the darkened jail. Buck lit a coal-oil lantern while Steves cursed out his pain, his wild, young shamed pride. Some of his fight returned as Buck jammed him inside the gamy-smelling cell.

"I won't be here long!" Steves shouted, furious.

Buck said: "You better hope that cowboy pulls through."

He was aware of a mixed relief and dread. He found himself thinking of Hetty Ahrens and discovered her beside Ma Price observing the milling crowd. He walked over and said: "I will see you home."

The older woman said: "Who is it this time?"

"Tip Steves shot a cowboy named Garr."

"Steves," Ma said knowingly, "is a Beeler man."

"Sounds about right." Buck nodded. He held his arm out to Hetty. They walked toward the river. There was a silence between them, but he didn't mind this. He could feel the damp coolness rising off the water as they paused before a house that stood silent and dark at the street's edge.

He spoke a low—"Good night."—and started to turn.

"So there will always be another town," she said, quietly condemning him, yet troubled for him in a way he had never noticed before in a woman.

"A man can't stop in the middle of the current," he said, "nor can he go back to where he began. I don't believe in mooning over what might have been."

She stood quite close, almost touching him. The nearness of her, faint and clean and sweet, drove a feeling around through the sap rising in him. She hadn't moved when his arms came up, reaching for her. Yet there was a holding back in him. She watched him, and he let his hands fall. He said— "Good night."—and left her.

He was filled with a terrible loneliness. He had thought for the briefest moment there had been a wanting in her, and then he'd remembered this was Crowder's woman. She was not for Buck Dancy, stained with violence and blood.

He had his place in this town, and went back to it—the hard-bright world of saloon row, rolling out the ugly sound of unsatisfied lusts. All along the slattern stretch these night noises placed their wild, insistent demand upon him and drew him on.

He put his shoulder to the Boomer's doors. Over by the poker tables Solomon Wight stood watching the play with Mack Rains at his side. Crowder was at the main table, gray-cheeked, morosely pondering his cards. Seeing Buck, Wight eased over. "Come on back," he said, waving Rains away, and Buck followed him into the office.

Wight said curtly, taking a bottle from the rolltop desk: "First crack out of the box you pistol-whip Kent Beeler's lieutenant. Haney's style." He poured two glasses.

Buck let his stand. "Haney's dead," he said.

"I heard."

"Well?" said Buck.

"Beeler will come brawling in here. You're too rough, Dancy."

Fire was leaping inside Buck. He said carefully: "Steves shot Johnny Garr."

"Garr will live. But Beeler will tear this town up by the roots. Let Steves go."

"To start something else?"

"Let 'em work off their cussedness."

"I can't see wild gun play."

Wight's eyes narrowed. "It's a short life and the gravy's thin. Could be something here for you each week."

The man was blunt enough, certainly. From the start Buck had known it would work around to this. "Wight," he said softly, "is that the best you can do?"

"I can break you!"

"I won't be caught like Charlie Stewart."

They stood there, glaring. Wight's furious stare broke first, and Buck, tight-mouthed, wheeled out of the room. His rashness growing, he elbowed over to the table where Crowder sat mired in his loser's dejection. The man was bent forward, in strain and frustration. He said angrily: "Damn the luck!" Suddenly he reared out of his kicked-back chair.

The house sharper, mouth curling, said: "Sol is particular about his I.O.U.s."

"He'll get his money!" Crowder flared. Jerking away, he

noticed Buck, and a surge of relief splashed across his face.

Buck nodded at the door. "Cooler out there."

Crowder, preceding him, attempted a swagger.

Outside, Buck said: "You can't beat Wight at his own game, Crowder."

"Wight's crooked!" Crowder snarled. "The whole town knows it!"

"Why play sucker, then?"

"Something ought to be done about him," Crowder said in a more thoughtful tone. He stood, silent and reflective, as though feeling his way through something important. "Maybe you could. . . ." He hesitated, peering at Buck.

"Could what?"

"Handle him . . . break him! Listen, I can. . . ."

Buck understood, for this, also, followed a similar pattern. "Get off the street," he said in disgust.

Crowder, shifting his boots, turned hurriedly away.

Watching the retreating shape, Buck worked this whole business over in his mind. Crowder was wild. He was weak. He owed Wight money for his gambling debts. He would like for Buck to stop Wight with a bullet.

A man, Adam Tipley, stepped into the light.

"You put a fast halter on Steves," he said. "Now what do you propose to do with him? There is no court here."

"If Garr doesn't pull through, I will take Steves to Pawnee for trial. But the doc thinks Garr will live. So Steves is the honey that draws Kent Beeler."

Tarpley said: "I was never one to horn in, Dancy. But Beeler's got twenty men. If you want help . . . ?"

Buck sighed. "Much obliged, Adam, only this ain't your worry." He left the man then, going on with his rounds. The solitary feeling was like a shadow at his shoulder.

Much later, in the straining light of early morning, he

watched the deadfalls disgorge their trade singly and in bunches. When the final whoop swelled and died and the Boomer's lights went dead, he tramped to the hotel.

He was taking his last look from the doorway, relishing this quiet, when a horse started up from the Pioneer barn. Wight's chunky shape bulked in the saddle. The man did not see Buck as he jogged toward the river. Another piece of Indian Rock's puzzle slipped into place for Buck.

This thinking was still with Buck, heavy and dark and cold-running, when he looked out from the lobby the following afternoon and saw Crowder going into the Boomer. Buck, watching him come out, read nervousness in the man's drawn face. Crowder headed directly across to Hetty Ahren's shop. Almost on the man's heels, Mack Rains shouldered out of the Boomer, drilling a glance at the shop before going down the street.

Buck found Wight at the Boomer's deserted bar, counting greenbacks into a black tin box. He did not look up.

Buck said: "You ride a fast horse."

"Don't you ever go to bed?" Wight demanded.

"I've seen it before," Buck told him tiredly. "Both ends against the middle. You and Beeler agree on how to break Steves loose?"

"I told him the straight of it."

"Your side. Where does Crowder figure in this?"

"Young Mister Crowder," Wight said savagely, "is in debt right up to his god-damn' ears. Three thousand dollars! He can't play here again until he pays up. But I can't have him running out on me. As for you"—Wight's hard piggish eyes came around—"you've gone too far. Beeler's riled. I won't be responsible."

"Still," Buck insisted, "it's you that's pulling him in." The cynical eyes told him nothing. "I'll be here. Steves stays in the jug."

Wight's back glance was button bright. He slapped the box shut and went into his office, slamming the door. Wight was pretty sure of himself.

Buck stepped back on the street. Beeler would come with darkness. Buck could sense the swift pull of events. He could die in this place. In this powdery street. In gun stink and blackness. Hetty Ahrens deepened his doubts. She was too much in his mind—why he'd held back. In this game a man had no business thinking of women.

The stale depression clawed at him, and he walked grimly to the shop. Crowder had gone. Buck sensed excitement in the girl.

"What does that man mean to you?" he said.

"He . . . well. . . ." She seemed uncertain, and then her chin tilted up. "He just asked me to marry him."

"A sensible man."

"He wants us to leave immediately. Oh, he's talked about leaving before this. There's nothing here for him. Perhaps in a new town. . . ."

"Sure," Buck nodded. *I wonder if he told her how much he owes Wight.* "You goin' with him?"

She tossed her head. Anger colored her cheeks. "We've got to go. He's being watched. I know he likes cards, but he'll make good what he owes. He promised me. . . . Can't you see? He's got no chance in this place. . . ."

She was loyal, Buck thought, loyal to a man who, expecting everything, gave nothing; and yet Buck wouldn't have changed her. "There's a way," he said, stringing out the thought. "After dark, I'll have two saddled horses behind the hotel. Ma Price can tell Crowder."

Her mouth parted. Her face changed, and what he saw

there he could not place, but he was stirred. She seemed unsure, and he hesitated to say more. When he did find words, she was looking away, and the moment, whatever it might have held, was gone.

"Thank you," she said.

He went out and walked to the Pioneer. He told Hap Spann—"Saddle two horses."—and felt a cold shock when Mack Rains came from the stall shadows, staring suspiciously, when Spann led the geldings out.

"One rider," Rains grunted. "Two horses."

Buck swung up.

Rains was a slow-thinking man. Yet, looking down, Buck could feel the backed-up surliness. Rains said: "Marshals ain't so tough."

"What do you know about marshals?"

"They all get it in time!"

"Ever been in Caldwell?"

"Go to hell," Rains said.

Buck turned the geldings and rode off.

Striking west, he thought of Charlie Stewart and Mike Haney, who had died the same way. Of Mack Rains and his killer's pride in his irons. Rains would be waiting somewhere in the shadows.

After an hour, Buck cut around to the southeast. Darkness lay across the rounded hills when he came to the shed in the alley. He got down, tied, and moved through the thick, warm blackness between the hotel and Crowder's office.

Pulled back in the gloom he watched riders fill the town, watched it emerge from its daytime shell for another headlong night. At the corner of his store Adam Tarpley stood with his silent dislike. In the corn-yellow light Solomon Wight, a chunkier shape, came through the winged lattices of the Boomer, stepping out to the walk's edge to drive his impatient look toward the ford. He jerked Tarpley a curt nod and strode back inside. Buck interpreted this byplay to mean Beeler was late.

All Buck's instincts came alive as he took in the wide-bodied man ranging up from the stables. Rains walked into the light and continued to search the street, up and down. Still looking, he drifted into a black wedge of shadow. At that, Tarpley wheeled and entered his store.

Silence ran on into the drag of minutes, and Buck heard the hotel's front door slap gently. Heavy steps made the planks creak. Ma Price stopped in front of him. "Hetty's waitin' out back." She stared at the street.

"Where's Crowder?"

"Holed up in his office. Buck, I don't like this. I don't like him. He's running. . . ."

"Hetty's problem. She wants to go."

Ma Price had scarcely moved her heavy body past him when a growing scuffle of horses came up from the river. The sound cut into him, and the riders showed in a black, bobbing wedge. They drummed up a swelling racket that bucketed hard along the street. They came at a gallop and pulled up in a tangle of dust before Wight's place. The man came out at once.

One of the riders called: "Where's that marshal?"

At that moment Crowder stepped out of his office. Sight of the horsemen seemed to freeze him. Buck's low call— "Over here!"—put him in motion, too obviously fleeing, his boots jarring racket from the boards.

"There he goes!" Rains shouted.

Crowder loomed suddenly near, breath coming in ragged gusts. "Back here!" Buck ordered, feeling the frantic fear in the man. Buck saw Hetty's blurred figure by the horses.

Only then did he know that all along he'd had the unreasoning hope she wouldn't go. Disappointment unleashed a recklessness in him. He wheeled and faced the street.

Directly behind him charged Rains, pistol lifting. Flame touched its tip, and lead slapped the wall at Buck's shoulder. Cool, Buck raised his arm and fired twice. He saw Rains stumble. Rains's hand strained upward, fell away. He made a small crying sound and dropped on his face.

"It's Dancy!"

Wight's furious voice lashed Beeler into action. As the outlaw reined his horse, Buck heard a drumfire of hoofs break out in the alley. He shifted position while he watched Beeler twist his head to stab a look through the darkness, watched Wight, abruptly bold, center his gun.

"Come out, Dancy!" Wight waggled the pistol. It was Beeler's signal to throw down, but he sat his horse like stone.

Buck stepped out. "Like when Rains shot Charlie Stewart in the back?" he called. "Like Mike Haney?"

Horses stomped, leather squeaked. He saw a man come out of Tarpley's store and stop on the porch.

In a flutter of movement Kent Beeler dropped his shoulder, bringing up his gun. Buck's pistol barked. Beeler's scream sheared through the reports. As Buck whirled toward Wight, knowing he was late, one loud blast overrode all sound. The gun fell from Wight's fist as he sagged.

Buck held his fire.

Heeling back on Beeler, he saw the outlaw with hands clapped across his chest. Shuddering, Beeler rolled out of the saddle.

Buck's glance raked across Beeler's muttering riders. They were beginning to press forward when a voice ripped their flanks: "Clear out!" Adam Tarpley ran from his porch with a shotgun. He swung the double barrels in a sweeping arc until they gave ground, until they began a retreat toward the dark river ford.

Afterward, Tarpley walked over to Wight's form. He tipped his head at Buck, who came across. "Meaning no disrespect for the dead," Tarpley said. "But Solomon Wight was too tough for this town."

Men gathered around, talking in subdued tones. Buck was filled with a powerful revulsion, with a solid weariness. Turning, he noticed Ma Price.

"Buck."

He kept gazing at her, watching Hetty Ahrens coming out of the shadows. Light touched her face, drawn tight, big-eyed. He started toward her.

"Arthur's gone. I sent him on."

She seemed to wait for him to speak, as she had that afternoon; and he knew that nothing in his life, before or after, could equal this moment. As he turned her away from the street, something in that motion told him that here, tonight, was his real beginning and Indian Rock his last town.

Comanche Woman

A brazen sun beat down on the figures strung out across the yellow prairie, their long travois poles raising puffs of smoky dust. They rode warily, on horses worn thin, as strangers in a land they had once known and claimed. They followed a single warrior toward the company of cavalry drawn up outside the stone fort.

"Think they mean trouble?" the young lieutenant in charge said nervously, turning to the weathered man whose ragged mustache drooped in its white oxbow over broad lips, whose getup struck the lieutenant as extremely outlandish for a government scout—greasy blue britches, calf-hide vest, calico shirt, and that ridiculous floppy hat banded with frayed beaver skin, worn as though a special mark or badge.

The old man—far older than he would admit to the officers at the fort—was shading one hand against the glare, squinting. He grew more intent, stiffly erect. His eyes weren't much by now, but he knew this band, these Antelope people. He watched the warrior leading them in. The broad, high-boned Comanche face, and the hair as fair as corn silk.

"No trouble," he replied after some moments, stifling the disgust he longed to express. "They wouldn't bring their families along an' start a fight. You're lookin' at the last Comanche band, Lieutenant. Remember that. Buff'lo's gone. The war's over." And a good deal more, he thought, his mind retreating suddenly to dwell on dim shapes and sunlit buttes and curly grasses that rolled away like an ocean, on these same whirlwind people and the dreaming white woman who had lived among them so long ago.

It was late afternoon, while the women gathered mesquite wood for the supper fires, before Emily could approach the small white girl brought in that morning as Kill Bears's captive.

The girl whirled, an instant fear climbing high in her small, taut face. "Let me be!" she cried, and shrank away. Her skin, too light for the Texas sun, had peeled on her nose and cheeks. Her hair was the color of flax and needed washing; even so, it managed to curl softly along the temples. But what held Emily rigid and aching was the terror she saw blazed in the thin face, in the enormous blue eyes that seemed too large for the rest of her. She was only nine or ten.

"No hurt . . . you," Emily said, forming the awkward words. Over the years she had made herself speak English so she would not forget how her people at the stockade had talked. She put out a tentative hand, and wasn't surprised when the girl struck it aside.

"No hurt . . . no hurt."

"Git away . . . you dirty Injun!" The girl snatched up her bundle of wood and ran.

Emily caught her easily. The captive whimpered and twisted, and in that brief struggle Emily felt a sickening knowledge. This little white girl wasn't strong enough for camp work. Not as Emily had been when captured. Once winter came she would die like a young quail caught in a blizzard.

"Me white . . . me white," Emily said, desperate to be understood, holding her firmly, but not hurting. She pointed to her own blue eyes and yellow hair. "See? Me white . . . like you."

The captive dropped her sticks. Some of her terror edged away, then suddenly all of it, as she seemed to notice Emily's features for the first time. Her mouth twisted, and she came sobbing into Emily's arms, and Emily was murmuring words she hadn't said in years.

"Your name, child?" she asked after a bit.

"Mary . . . Mary Tabor."

"Where is your home?"

"Down river from Fort Belknap."

"That's on the Salt Fork of the Brazos."

Mary displayed a small, pleased, wet-eyed smile. "You've been there?"

"A long time ago," Emily lied, wanting to humor her.

"My folks . . . ," Mary began, and trailed off, lips quivering.

Emily shook her head. "Don't talk now. Go back to camp. Don't let the Indians see you crying. Be brave."

That evening she spoke to Jumping Bull. "The little *Tejano* girl Kill Bears captured. I want her for a slave in our lodge."

"She is not strong. You would have to take care of her."

"She's not strong now because Kill Bears is mean to her. She goes hungry. She longs for her people. I could teach her many things. She will grow strong. She will be like a little sister to me."

Across the soft gloom in the teepee, Emily saw her husband's dark gaze play over her; it gave her a warm feeling. She could not forget how he had paid Runs Antelope, her captor, many horses for her. She was proud of him, in a way. Jumping Bull was a rising warrior who never lacked followers when he led war parties against the Utes or *Tejanos*. And even when she knew he was raiding the settlements, she wanted him to return. She wondered why, as a wealthy man who had only one son, he hadn't taken another woman into his lodge. A skilled hunter, he could provide for several wives and many children.

But for her, always, between them, lay the wedge of her massacred people, so distant and lost in time they might never have existed save in a dream, even though he had been too young to go on that raid.

He didn't answer, and she, wanting this as nothing she had asked before, wisely forced down her eagerness.

Two days passed. Then she noticed that Jumping Bull's horse herd appeared smaller. Certain swift buffalo runners were missing. She said nothing and waited.

On the third day Mary Tabor came to live in the lodge.

"Now tell me about your kinfolks," Emily said.

Mary stared at the toe of her rawhide moccasin. "Wiped out. 'Less Uncle Amos got away." She shuddered, and Emily saw the fear again, livid as a quirt slash in the pale face.

"Someday you will go back," Emily said gravely, sad for her. "Don't ever quit hopin'. I ain't."

Mary's large eyes showed a searching, inquisitive look, older than her years. "Mean you'd leave Jumping Bull if you could?"

Emily averted her eyes, somehow annoyed and surprised.

"He's mighty good for an Injun," Mary went on. "Gave good horses for me. He ain't mean like Kill Bears, who beats his womenfolks. Reckon I'm lucky . . . I know that. And you . . . you're so good to me, Emily. Now you show me how to do Injun chores. I got to earn my keep. I can sew a mite. I can cook. I can make cornbread."

"There's no corn meal," Emily said, smiling, knowing Mary would be no bother. First, she washed and braided

Mary's light hair; by that afternoon she had lost the driven look. Soon Emily dressed her in buckskins, after working the hides until they were soft and smooth and buff in color, and adding bright bead designs and fringes on sleeves and hems.

Having Mary close and hearing her speech awakened in Emily sleeping words and expressions. Homesickness seized her. She saw as never before the cool spring beyond the stockade where the children had played, the red plum bushes heavy with fruit, the sweet, dim faces of her mother and the neighbor women. She thought of her father, away when the Indians struck. Was he alive? Had he searched for her or offered ransom? She felt the strength of a new determination. She spent more time instructing Yellow Bird, her son.

"Peace is better than war," she would say when Jumping Bull wasn't around. "It is not right to kill."

"*Tejanos* kill us," the boy said. He was brown as any Comanche, and he had the proud, high cheek bones of his father, but you couldn't mistake the white cast of his mouth, or the blue eyes and yellow hair. Trouble was, he thought like a Comanche.

"It takes a brave man to follow the peace road," she said, "when the others howl to fight."

The boy looked puzzled. "My father is brave. He fights."

When they reached a stopping place in their discussions, he would leap up with relief and run out. Emily, left to her dreaming, could see him grown up as a white man and living in a wooden house with windows.

By the time the band trailed out on the vast prairie floor of the Staked Plains for summer trading, she was thinking of home with an increasing sick desperation. Her resolve deepened.

They drew up to a place called *Casas Amarillas*—the Yellow Houses—a high bluff in which caves had been cut.

There the Comancheros waited with their familiar high-wheeled *carretas*.

Emily's usual excitement was missing. She moved dully. Mary helped her raise the long cedar teepee poles and lift the cover of dressed buffalo skins against the framework, fasten the small wooden pins, and pound the pegs. That done, Mary joined the other youngsters curiously observing the trade people and the many bright goods.

Soon she came flying back. "There's a white man out there!"

"White man!" Emily looked up. "No white man has ever come here." She shook her head; it wasn't possible.

"He's a trader," Mary insisted, impressed, and her hands framed the shape of a large man. "Black boots . . . buckskins, and a big round hat with beaver skin around it. The children call him Beaver Hat."

Emily got up. "He's white? You're certain?"

"I heard him talkin' to Jumping Bull. I saw him as close as I am to you."

"Then he will come here," Emily said, more to herself. There would be much palavering and smoking and feasting before Jumping Bull, who owned more horses than any warrior in the band, struck his trade. Excitement swept her.

To her disappointment, Jumping Bull returned alone. He looked pleased and secretive as he reached inside his blanket and held out something that shone.

She caught her breath. It was a silver necklace, turquoise set in each link, very bright and pretty in the sun; his first real gift to her, worth many horses. She considered it longingly, in confusion. She took the necklace and spread it out in her hands, and started to slip it over her head. As she did, a thought arrested her. Jumping Bull didn't know she was going to tell the trader about her people. Therefore, it would be unseemly for her to wear his gift. Yet she couldn't refuse it.

"It's too pretty to wear now," she said, instead, and saw the flicker of hurt deep in his brown eyes before he walked away.

Afterward, she placed the necklace among her things— with the hand mirror, the colored beads left over from making Mary's dress, awls and needles of sharpened bone, a pair of thin, shell earrings obtained from the Comancheros, and a broken comb found in the litter of an old campground.

Near evening the next day she took a buffalo paunch to the water hole below the yellowish cliffs. Coming back, she looked about and stopped suddenly. Tiny tremors raced through her.

A raw-boned white man in a broad hat was walking beside Jumping Bull. She delayed, until they passed her and entered the lodge. Had the white man noticed her pale skin? Her yellow hair?

She hung up the water paunch, and, when she came to the lodge door, carrying a kettle of meat, she paused desperately so Beaver Hat could see her framed there in the full light. Going in, she saw her husband on his robes, facing the door. Beaver Hat sat on his left, in the place of honor. She lingered so long while placing the kettle and wooden bowls and spoons that Jumping Bull threw her a questioning look.

Beaver Hat seemed not to notice.

She stood outside, slumped in dejection. As a Comanche woman she couldn't approach the white man in camp. People would laugh at Jumping Bull, whose wife talked to strangers. Yet why should she, a captive, think of him and his reputation as a warrior? She didn't understand herself.

Yellow Bird ran in to eat. She fed him and watched him run off into the dusky light. She sent Mary to play and sat motionless, listening to the murmuring voices inside the teepee. A thought settled, it kept growing, stirring her. She emptied the paunch into a large kettle and went unhurriedly to the spring and opened the bag, letting it fill slowly while she watched.

When she could wait no longer, when evening's haze masked the brown land and her long absence would be noted, she saw a figure leave the lodge and start toward the trader's camp.

She rose at once, the water bag forgotten, and stepped away, striding to intercept him. But the fine feeling of anticipation with which she had begun deserted her suddenly. She slowed her step, uncertain. What if he pretended again not to see her?

She could hear his boot steps, heavy, steady. Not once did his head turn in her direction. His gaze seemed fixed afar. His beaver hat made him look taller.

She walked faster and turned to stand across his path. He couldn't miss her now! She saw his eyes stray over her, and she waited for some sign that she existed. He came on, just a few steps away. Still, he gave no awareness of her.

Her head lifted. She was white, not Comanche! She posted herself squarely. Facing him, she saw him swing his glance left and right. To her astonishment and relief, he halted and said, low: "I know, ma'am . . . you're white." She heard nothing but pity as he spoke, pity and helplessness.

She touched her breasts. "Me Emily . . . Emily Bragg," she said, and suddenly she became angry with herself. She had thought so long over the impressive way she would speak, the rehearsed white man's words. Now, in her anxiety, she was falling back on the old, halting, Indian-camp English, which she'd come to despise since Mary came.

"Bragg? Bragg?" He pulled on his chin and mulled the name around on his tongue. He shifted one high shoulder and inclined his head in the manner of one who listens. A tawny mustache fell down the slopes of his broad mouth. His eyes, almost white against the brownness of his face, squinted in at the corners. The eyes were wise, but missing was the shrewd glint of a Comanchero.

"My father's name was Josiah Bragg. He built a fort on a river." She could never think of him as dead; at last the words were rising off her tongue. "The settlers called it Fort Bragg. There was a massacre . . . ever'body killed. . . ."

"On the Navasota, wasn't it?" he interrupted, and nodded reminiscently, in sympathy. "I recollect that. You been all this time with the Antelope-Eaters?"

"Since I was ten."

He hesitated, not meeting her eyes. "They didn't swap you off none . . . nor trade you around to other bands or tribes?"

"No," she replied, and drew herself straighter.

He appeared relieved, although his pity slid back as he said: "Now you're Jumping Bull's woman?"

"*His wife,*" she said, surprised at her instant sharpness. "Listen to me! I still have people. I know. They'll pay ransom."

"Thought you said everybody was rubbed out?"

"My father wasn't there. He was east in the settlements." She spoke in a torrent, in confusion, and a pang of guilt pressed her. She'd meant to tell him first about Mary. "Listen! There's a little *Tejano* girl here . . . Mary Tabor. Her folks lived on the Brazos Salt Fork. Maybe she's got kin left . . . somebody. The pony soldiers at Fort Belknap will know. Somebody'll remember that raid . . . just last summer. Her folks had stock." Emily didn't know whether Mary's people possessed wealth or not; as she remembered, everybody on the frontier was poor. She'd said that on impulse; anything to

50

stir up the greed in this white trader who didn't look or act like a Comanchero. "Her people, my people, I know will pay ransom. Many guns, many blankets."

"What about your boy?" he asked. "Figure Jumping Bull'd give up you an' the boy together?"

She shook her head evasively and touched his arm with a pleading gesture. "All I know is I've dreamed about goin' home ever since they took me. You will take word?"

She waited, feeling her throat muscles tighten. Waves of purple twilight thickened across the open land and lay banked in darker shadows against the foot of the bluff. Camp sounds fell away.

"Ma'am," he said, finally, "true, I brought some trade goods. But no guns. I ain't a real Comanchero. I'm a scout for the State of Texas. There's a big war comin' between the States." When her brows knitted in puzzlement, he tried to explain and pointed. "Americans ag'in' Americans. North and South. A brother-killin' war. Mighty bad. Texas wants to keep the Comanches peaceful. That's why I'm here."

"You take word?" she said, slipping into the sparse, hated camp lingo.

He didn't answer at once. "I'll try. Maybe I can locate somebody. If I can, I'll send a rider back. My man can say the *Tejanos* are lookin' for two whites like you an' Mary. That there'll be ransom goods." She was thanking him with her eyes, her throat too full for speech. "Ma'am, you're a mighty brave woman. Only don't get your hopes too high now. If I can't find anybody . . . well. Could be, too, the band won't let you go."

"I am Jumping Bull's *wife*," she said. "Not *their* slave."

Beaver Hat's eyes looked thoughtful, but Emily no longer saw pity. He had that expression as he walked off.

Emily clung to it, trusting it, as the slow days wore away

and the fickle band shifted from one scattered watering to another. By late summer, as restless as the whirlwinds that played across their shimmering world, the Antelope-Eaters had returned to the Yellow Houses, where the constant *roo-roo-oo* of bellowing buffalo bulls meant winter meat ranged nearby.

That was when the dark-skinned rider found them. Emily felt the hot clutch of excitement as she gave him food and fought down her questions. Was her father alive? Was Mary's uncle?

The rider and Jumping Bull talked, and then the man went to his picketed horse and waited.

It seemed a long time before Jumping Bull called her, before she stood in the gloom of the lodge. She had never feared him. Except now she had to will herself to meet his eyes.

"Beaver Hat," he said, expressionless, "sends me word from the *Tejano* chiefs. They want to buy you and the little white slave."

She stared into her hands, ashamed for him to see her naked elation.

"Your home is here," he told her.

"I am not Comanche," she said, looking up. "I want to go back to my people."

"It would not be the same. Your skin is white, but your heart is Comanche."

"I am a white woman. I want my son to live as a white man."

His dark eyes flashed a baffled anger.

"My father is rich. He will pay much for me."

He flinched as if struck. His eyes locked on her, in them something she had never seen until now. He strode past her, gone.

White-faced, standing by the lodge door, she saw him go

out and speak to the rider. What was he saying?

He told her nothing, and the following morning, taking only his medicine bundle, he rode off alone. He returned after three days, lean and hollow-eyed.

Soon she heard the camp crier calling: "You friends of Jumping Bull . . . come to his lodge tonight. He will lead a war party against the Utes."

Emily's heart turned cold. In that moment she became a Comanche woman again, fearing for her warring husband. She watched with dread as the warriors hung up their shields to absorb the powerful sun medicine and readied weapons. All except Jumping Bull, who chose only his long *bois d'arc* lance, which only the bravest carried. A war lance man never retreated, and the feeling spread through her that he would not return.

All during the hot afternoon she heard him singing and drumming songs in the lodge. Near sundown the war party paraded through the village. They would leave tonight, for it was bad to go in daylight.

As darkness fell, the old men beating the drums struck up a throbbing song. Now the departing warriors began choosing women partners for the dance.

Emily waited. Always before he had danced with her.

His gaze brushed her, just once. He wheeled swiftly by. That was all. He danced on, and she knew that he had shut her out of his heart.

Living was dreading and dreaming and instructing young Yellow Bird. *Is it good to see friends in their grief, slashing themselves? Is it good to see old people without sons, no one to kill meat for them? Is the war way good?*

Several times a day she climbed the bluff to catch the first signs of distant movement, hoping to see low puffs of dust, or dark figures crawling through the glazy heat waves.

On the afternoon that she sighted the bobbing shapes in the west, she thought first of the war party. She watched a long time; they were so far away and the sun burned her eyes.

Of a sudden she dropped her head. There was no war party. The figures out there were mainly mules pulling high-wheeled carts. But remembering Mary, she felt a warm triumph, and she ran toward camp.

They stood outside the lodge and waited for Beaver Hat to make his way through the Comanches swarming around the carts. He came quickly. As he approached, Emily took Mary's hand.

"It's all right," he announced, displaying the engulfing smile of one bringing good news. "Got plenty of things . . . blankets, calico, tobacco, coffee, kettles."

Mary uttered a small cry, and Emily held her harder.

"Ma'am," Beaver Hat said, his eyes fixing Emily alone, "your father is still living. There's a little town growed up there now close to the fort."

Emily felt her throat lump. A mist crossed her eyes. She fought a sudden trembling. "Is . . . is he old?" she asked, and the fort and its phantom people and the Navasota and its post-oak hills swam in a sweet haze. "I mean . . . does he look old?" In truth, she didn't know what she meant.

"His hair is snow white. A hardy man for his age, though. Handles stock. Raises cotton. He's well to do."

"Did he . . . is he?" Again, Emily faltered.

"He never married again, if that's what you mean. Lives by himself. He wants you back, ma'am. Says you're all he's got. He's never quit lookin' for you." His voice changed. "I figure we'd better pull out tomorrow."

Emily didn't understand. She stared into his face. "Pull out? My husband is making war on the Utes." She hesitated even more, and, when she spoke, her voice sounded other than her own. "And my son?" Her gaze broke away from his.

"Mean Jumping Bull didn't tell you?" he demanded, astonished. "Why, he gave his word to my man last summer. You can go home now. You an' Mary. With me. As for the boy, it's his choice to go or stay. What's more, Jumping Bull didn't' want any ransom goods. Your father sent 'em just the same . . . for good will."

"My husband is gone," she said again dully. "I can't go now. His war party's been out a long time."

Beaver Hat pulled on his beard, and she could see the wise eyes thoughtfully upon her. He said: "That's not all. About that fight on the Salt Fork, ma'am. All Mary's kin got wiped out. I'm mighty sorry."

Mary's fingers were clawing into Emily's palm. But Mary didn't whimper as she would have months ago.

"Now, ma'am," he said earnestly, "set your mind to this. I can wait a few days. No longer. I won't ever be back here again." He turned away.

Emily heard shouts on the afternoon of the second day after Beaver Hat's arrival. She ran out to the shrillness of wailing voices, and, hurrying to the camp's edge, she recognized a warrior who had traveled with the war party. His face was painted black. Scattered behind him trailed a small band of riders. Sixteen men had gone to war; not half that many were returning. Jumping Bull, she saw, wasn't among them.

She stumbled. The sky was spinning. As she swayed upward, she noticed, just now, the cedar-pole travois.

Running, running, she found him upon it. His long spear lay beside him, unbroken. A red, wicked slash ran crookedly across his chest. His dark eyes, open, took no notice of her even when she bent over him. She heard a warrior say: "He counted many coups with the war lance before he went down. He told us to leave him, but we put him on the drag. His spirit wants to stay in his body, but his heart is on the ground."

She followed them, holding herself tightly, as if she might fall apart if she did not, followed as they carried him inside the lodge. Seeing him on the buffalo robes, she thought: *He tried to die . . . only he was too strong, too brave.* And she was proud.

Yellow Bird sat at his warrior father's feet to watch and worship. Mary Tabor, big-eyed, silent, slipped to Emily's side, intent on the rise and fall of Jumping Bull's heavy breathing. And in the wide eyes Emily saw again the fear that Mary had when she first came to the Indian camp.

In a little while Emily felt Mary touch her arm. She turned to find Beaver Hat standing back from the doorway. Emily stepped outside, Mary close on her heels.

"I saw them bring him in," Beaver Hat said, nodding his regret. He paused. "I'll have to know now, ma'am. Hard time for you to decide. I understand that."

Emily felt Mary's hand creep inside hers, and the calling images of her father and the fort and the people seemed to float again before her, revealed in soft sunlight, forever there, forever secure. She could see each face, each remembered woodland path and hill shape.

"No harder," she said then, shaking her head. "Guess I decided the other day . . . just didn't know. My home is here." And suddenly: "But Mary will go! My father is old . . . she will make him a good daughter."

At that, Mary sobbed, and Emily felt her fierce, small grasp.

Beaver Hat's jaw hung. His broad lips opened, closed. His eyes ran over her, thoughtfully, a blend of sadness behind them. And he did a strange thing. He swept off his hat. For her, she knew, some *Tejano* sign she didn't remember. But she sensed it was good, and without pity.

Mary couldn't stop sobbing. "Emily, don't make me leave you!"

Emily grew firm. She took Mary's arm, just as she had that first day, and led her the few steps to Beaver Hat.

"Go now . . . be brave," Emily said, and kissed one wet cheek. "Don't look back. I don't think I could stand that."

She watched them walk off. Once Mary seemed to lag, to falter, to cry. But she didn't look back.

Emily turned. She went inside and searched among her scant possessions and found the necklace, which she looped around her neck.

She saw Jumping Bull look up as she faced around. His dark, warm gaze came over her.

"There will never be another woman in this lodge," he said.

She inclined her head, indicating approval. The faces in the old dream had gone. Only those of her husband and son were real. Yet, for Yellow Bird, because he was young, she could dream of the peace road.

Face of Danger

Terrell Kinder rose from his chair by the rolltop desk and made a restless circle around the log-walled room. He did not know when the day had gone wrong for him, but somehow it had. He returned to the desk, his high boot heels resounding in the empty house, and stared down with distaste at the pile of thick ranch ledgers. Stirred by a deep discontent, he turned to the elkhorn rack to reach for his hat.

A moment later he dropped his hand. There was no time today for loping across country with old Fargo, his ranch hand. Reluctantly he sat down with the records again, but his mind was wandering. Then he heard a horse hammer across the yard and stop quickly.

Terrell winced. Only one man rode in such a punishing fashion—Ennis Buell, the Indian agent at War Bonnet. Buell pushed open the door and came abruptly inside, not bothering to knock. Irritation touched Terrell, not so much at the absence of manners as at the man himself, with his infernal brusqueness. Then he relented as quickly. It was a small thing; any other day Terrell wouldn't have minded.

"A drink?" he offered, rising.

"Too early in the day." Buell was well-dressed for this part of the territory, almost dapper in dove-gray shirt, string tie, and broadcloth coat. He was a man of about thirty, several years younger than Terrell, slender and yet hard-knit, his neck thick and his hands strong and quick.

Terrell could not help recalling the simple, dedicated Quaker agent whom Buell had succeeded, and instantly decided the comparison was unfair. Buell had proved himself efficient in tribal range matters.

"Drumming up some late lease bidders?" Terrell asked.

"Hardly necessary," Buell answered in his blunt manner. "Out checking tribal range. No, you'd be bidder enough to take over Gibb Shepherd's lease. Not that he won't make some sort of bid himself. He's eager to renew, since it's his salt and bacon."

"It would be, if he managed well," said Terrell, with a trace of old heat.

"Shouldn't be hard for you to top his bid. Shepherd's near broke, and you have one of the best ranches going." Buell smiled briefly. "Naturally, your high figure will please me."

"The sky's the limit," Terrell said curtly. "I'll beat anything Shepherd offers. I haven't forgotten a few things . . . like missing beef."

"You're coming in to the agency, then?"

Terrell nodded, wondering why Buell even asked. "I'll be in town till the sale's over. But my attorney, Bert McGrath, will bid me in. I'm shunning the agency today. . . ." Terrell caught himself. He'd spoken the last without thinking, not aware until now that he intended to avoid Shepherd.

"Oh?" A flicker of surprise showed in Buell's freshly shaven face.

"It's easier. I don't hunt trouble."

"Of course not. But for a man of your reputation as a fighter. . . ."

"I'd hate to shoot Shepherd," explained Terrell matter-of-factly. "I had my fill of gun play some years ago."

"That was before my time," said Buell, quietly interested.

"Yes. We cleaned out these hills good. We shot and hanged some cow thieves, and some we sent to the pen . . . men like Nels Ivy, who really deserved hanging, too." Terrell broke off, annoyed to find himself speaking of certain long-buried events in which he took no personal pride.

"This Ivy," Buell asked casually, "was he much of a man?"

"Tough, if you mean that. Real handy with a gun." Terrell stopped. He'd talk no more of the past.

Buell appeared to sense it. He stepped briskly to the door. "Three o'clock at the agency," he reminded, going out.

"McGrath knows. He'll be there."

Coming out to the rambling porch, cool and shaded under the blazing sun, Terrell watched Buell mount and ride off at a hard gallop.

Old Fargo loomed near, a thin, gaunt figure, like a relic from the savage days of the past. Terrell knew the old watchdog had been posted outside all the time, in needless vigilance, ready if called.

With hawk's eyes, old Fargo squinted after Buell. "Poor way to treat horseflesh," he snorted.

Terrell smiled without speaking. An affection linked them, although it was never mentioned. "We're going to town pretty soon," Terrell announced, and went inside to wrestle with the ledgers again.

An hour later, he picked his hat off the horns and by habit reached for the worn cartridge belt, oiled holster, and pistol. Settling them to his lank hips with wide-knuckled hands, his morning's depression returned. He didn't like what he saw of himself this moment—a leftover from the sudden, violent times, maybe outgrowing his own usefulness.

In early afternoon, seeing War Bonnet below in a fold of the limestone hills, Terrell had a sweeping view of this rolling grass country. It still looked largely open, but he noted more windmills and houses now in the distance, and fences pressing a man in. He'd made a small fortune here, in the space of ten years after leaving Texas, buying range when he could, leasing from the Indian reserves, and fighting when necessary, during the stormy beginning. Of late, more Texans had moved in, and more trainloads of Lone Star cattle headed north each year to summer and winter upon the lush graze.

Yet, glancing at old Fargo, who still packed his single-action pistol, Terrell realized most of the fun had gone. Now, in the inflexible old man riding beside him, he could see Terrell Kinder in the coming years—alone, a Spanish horse penned tight, still unruly, still fighting the bit and, therefore, doomed because of it.

They stabled their horses at Joel Creed's livery and started up the plank walk, past the wagon yard, toward the Cattle King Hotel. Old Fargo roved his suspicious gaze along the street, across the scattering of tied saddle horses before the hitching racks.

"Never did like the smell of this town," he growled.

"We can wait at the hotel," Terrell said, "till McGrath buys that lease."

Old Fargo paced on before he spoke. "I've never been much of a hand to tell a man his own game. But are you sure we need more range, Terrell?"

"Why not? We can use it. It's good business."

"Business!" Old Fargo shook his head. "Everything's sure cold business these days, isn't it? There's no fight or frolic left any more."

"The old days are gone," Terrell admitted. "We both know it."

Old Fargo's head snapped up. "Trouble is . . . does the other fellow? I've seen men get killed for less than a lease."

Each seemed to let the talk die by common consent, but Terrell knew Fargo hadn't finished his say. As they came back to the hotel entrance, Fargo pulled back. "You go ahead. I believe I'll visit around."

Before Terrell could protest, old Fargo had turned and was walking up the street.

His sudden leaving disturbed Terrell. Frowning, he entered the hotel lobby. A voice calling his name—a woman's voice—made him glance around.

Leigh Richmond stood just a step beyond, a slim-bodied young woman whose full lips and frank eyes were smiling at him. Her father was Colonel DeWitt Richmond, a Texas cattleman who had come here to live during the past year.

"I've been waiting for you," said Leigh Richmond, taking his arm.

"Waiting?"

"Yes. I knew you'd be in town. Lease day, isn't it?"

He stared. It struck him as a little odd. "So it is. But. . . ."

Her hand tightened. "Terrell, I have to talk to you."

"That serious, is it?" he asked, chuckling. "My pleasure. Do you want to talk here?"

"Upstairs. Father's there."

Around her he felt different, changed. Her presence always affected him keenly. He sensed a feeling between them and knew he'd delayed too long, somehow unsure of himself.

When they entered the room, Colonel Richmond, tall and angular, rose to shake hands. "Glad to see you, Terrell. I've business to attend to, Leigh. You'll have to excuse me. Terrell, we don't see enough of you. You must be working too hard."

"There's a lot to do, Colonel."

"Most of it will keep. When you reach my age, you'll understand." Colonel Richmond studied Terrell a moment and seemed uncomfortable. "Please be considerate of Leigh. I'm aware that she speaks out of turn." He left the room.

Curious, Terrell turned to find Leigh appraising him uncertainly. She stood rather tall, and her straight blue-black hair, knotted at the nape of her neck, accented the smoky grayness of her wide-set eyes. Her mouth was firm, yet full and alive below the rounded contours of her high cheeks.

She was no halfway woman, he thought, admiring her. Strong-willed, she had a moving, inner sweetness—and also a capacity for temper and scorn, if need be. Seeing her thus, he wondered why he'd held back from her.

"Father's right," she said. "It's none of my business."

He understood suddenly. "You mean the lease?"

"Yes. Is it so important to you, Terrell?"

"The land's not Shepherd's," he replied steadily. "It's Indian graze, open to the highest bidder."

"I know that. But it's his living. If he loses it, he's out of business."

"He can bid for it, can't he?"

"He doesn't stand a chance against you. You know that."

He admitted it silently, and held his tongue.

"Oh, Terrell, you're a big man. He's small . . . always will be, I suppose. I want you to stay big . . . in yourself."

"Leigh, there's one thing maybe you don't know about." His voice grew harsh. "Shepherd's a thief, a common cow thief."

She met his gaze, quiet and searching. "You have proof?"

"The association checked him. He served time in Kansas."

"I mean," she persisted, "that he stole your cattle?"

"I never missed stock till he leased next to me. It fits pretty close."

"But you aren't sure."

He spoke fast, impatiently. "There's not enough proof to bring charges, but I've lost several steers. My men found horns and bones. He's just a rawhide rancher. We used to shoot his kind before there was any law. I don't want him near my range."

Feeling flashed across her face. She stepped forward, lifting a slim, restraining hand, until she stood very close and he caught her faint, heady fragrance. "Terrell, please! Didn't it ever occur to you that was why he left Kansas . . . to start over again, here, in the territory? Please, listen. Last winter I stayed with Missus Shepherd when she had her last baby. They've nothing, not a thing. The freeze just about wiped them out."

"Every rancher lost cattle," Terrell said coldly. "Shepherd's just a poor manager, that's all. And if he was so hard put, why didn't he speak up? We'd have all helped . . . even me."

Her face turned soft, her large eyes pleading. "I'd never have known if I hadn't happened by his ranch. You have your pride, and Gibb Shepherd has his. Perhaps he was too proud to ask for help."

"There was no need to, you mean, when he could live off his neighbor's stock."

Her long fingers dug into his arms. "You don't understand, do you, Terrell? I'm trying to keep you from doing something you'll regret the rest of your life . . . if you turn that family out."

"You make it sound brutal, Leigh. But I can't bow under. A thief's a thief."

"Terrell," she said, shaking her dark head, "you can't."

"Look here, Leigh," he answered impatiently, "I refuse to let this come between us. I've fooled around long enough." He took her by the shoulders, and the touch of her ripped through him. "I own a big ranch, a big house, but it's empty. It needs a woman. Let me take you to it. Then we'll travel the country . . . Saint Louis, New Orleans, New York."

Almost imperceptibly, he felt her stiffen. "Is that what you think I'd like, Terrell? A great ranch, a good time, nothing more?"

"Why. . . ." Taken aback, he strained to speak. The unaccustomed words seemed to stick in his throat. "That's just part of it," he said awkwardly. "I . . . you know. . . ."

Leigh Richmond shook off his hands. "Last night a man rode out to the ranch. He told me he loved me, and he asked me to marry him."

"Who?" His anger flared up before he could stamp it out. "Who dared say that?"

"I'll never tell you." She appeared to grow taller, defiant and scornful. "Because if I did, you'd kill him!"

"Did he kiss you . . . like this?"

In a single step he reached out and took her, his arms rough. He kissed her hard, forcing her head back. She made no resistance, but neither did she meet his lips. Her body felt like so much putty in his arms.

He released her and stood back, suddenly shamed. He continued to stare at her, jarred by a sudden realization. He'd want to break any man who touched her and took her from him, and yet violence would never work with her. Now all his anger was gone, and he felt only a shaken humbleness, which he could not express to her for the life of him. Slowly, without speaking, he found his hat and went to the door.

"Terrell."

He turned and heard her ask in the quietest of voices: "Is that all you intend to tell me?"

"It is. I know where I stand now."

He opened the door, and again her voice pulled at him.

"You're going through with the lease?"

He gave a quick nod.

"Terrell," she said coldly, "for obvious reasons, no man has ever told you what you are . . . what you've become. But I will, even though it's too late." She was trembling. She took a deep breath and said firmly: "You're hard and unforgiving. You came here when a man had to fight to exist, when it was kill or be killed. But while other men changed later, you didn't. You're still back there in those dreadful times. You always will be. I'm truly sorry to say this, but there's no place for a man like you any more."

He accepted it in silence, head bowed. What really shook him, however, was the realization of what he'd lost in losing Leigh.

She stood with both hands clenched on the table edge. She looked tall and very straight, her loveliness made still greater because it lay forever beyond him now. He felt a bottomless regret.

"Well, Leigh," he said, turning, "you told me. I wish you happiness."

He shouldered through the doorway, went downstairs, and found himself outside, standing on the plank walk, in the grip of a terrible loneliness.

Grit blew along the street, stinging his face. The wind off the hills was wild. You can't go back, he thought; the only thing constant is change. It had required a big part of his life to learn that, to see himself as he actually was.

His gaze lifted. Across the street Bert McGrath's office sign swayed in the wind. He rolled a brown paper cigarette, his mind tightening as he eyed the sign. He hardly noticed when a passing rider spoke. Suddenly he crushed the cigarette between his fingers and strode toward McGrath's law office.

Terrell missed something as he entered the office—McGrath's usual hearty greeting. McGrath, a heavy-set man with a mane of white hair, frowned from behind his desk. He raised his eyes and got to the point immediately.

"Still aim to buy the Shepherd lease?"

"Certainly. Why do you ask?"

"Figured you might change your mind, maybe ease up on him. Shepherd's had a hard year."

Terrell's jaw firmed. "You're the association attorney, Bert. You know why I'm after that lease."

"Yes," McGrath answered wearily, "I reckon I do. But. . . ."

"What are you trying to tell me, Bert?" Terrell demanded, leaning forward. "That I should abide a thief?"

Scowling, McGrath heaved to his feet and paced to the window overlooking Main Street. He studied it a space, then spoke, almost to himself. "It wouldn't be so bad if he could get another lease. But he can't. All the small tracts are spoken for, and he can't handle the fee on a larger one."

"I've known men to lose every head of cattle in a blizzard and still survive."

McGrath said: "You could, in the old days. It's different now." His voice changed, grew harsher. "Terrell, this is the first time I ever knew you to misjudge a man."

"My mind is made up, Bert."

McGrath's shrug was a mixture of resignation and disappointment. "Ah, so it is." He settled his eyes upon Terrell, who wondered why he should feel unease under the steady gaze.

"See you after the sale," Terrell said abruptly, and stepped to the door.

To his surprise, the older man followed him several steps. "Buell tells me he expects just two bids, yours and Shep-

herd's. To me that means the other ranchers are laying off . . .
to give Shepherd a lift, maybe. Or else they don't want to
buck Terrell Kinder. Reckon you've become quite a big man,
Terrell."

Terrell jerked to a stop, on the verge of a hot reply. But
Bert McGrath was already pacing back to his desk, and
Terrell locked the words inside him, feeling a surge of shame.
Had he come to this, brawling with long-standing friends just
because they held differing opinions?

Outside, he looked up and down the dusty street for old
Fargo, and, not sighting him, he started a slow stroll. A wave
of loneliness came, and he could not shake it. The two bids
told the story, he realized. Men feared him, and the knowledge hurt. For he liked the company of most men, in his silent
way. Nonetheless, a man was judged by his actions. Suddenly
he knew a harsh truth: those violent times had marked him, as
Leigh had said. They'd forced him into a taciturn shell. He
wasn't liked.

Walking slowly, he thought of old Fargo and his dogged,
loyal service, and felt a deep gratefulness. Looking back,
Terrell knew Fargo had excused a great deal and had overlooked his temper and pride and bluntness. As for Leigh
Richmond, he'd blindly allowed her to slip away to another
man—a mistake he'd remember for the rest of his days. And
there was Bert McGrath. Their friendship would never be the
same.

"Howdy, Mister Kinder."

Terrell glanced up at a man in worn range clothes, one
Frank Pruitt, a tolerable good horse breaker who'd drifted
too much, seldom staying in one place.

"I just wondered," ventured Pruitt, "if you still have a full
crew out your way?"

Terrell's first response was to remind Pruitt that a rider

looking for work always came to the office in the rambling log house. He said—"It's been quiet lately."—and then he heard himself saying: "No, there is a job. You might ride out tomorrow. Rolly Harvick's getting himself married."

As he spoke, a strange embarrassment engulfed him. He passed on quickly, before Pruitt could see it. Yet, in that brief interval, Terrell read another damning reflection of himself. Pruitt's sunburned face mirrored a great surprise, and Terrell understood. Pruitt had expected rebuff, and only his obvious need had driven him to approach Terrell Kinder on the street.

Terrell spun around. His voice carried the old bite. "Remember, if you work for me, there'll be no damned drifting once your belly's full!"

Pruitt nodded fast, murmuring his thanks, and Terrell walked on. Already he regretted his impulsive action, because Pruitt wouldn't stay long. It came to him that yesterday he'd have turned Pruitt down. He guessed he'd been touched by Pruitt's watery eyes, which showed a certain hunger.

Thinking of old Fargo again, he moved to the street's end. Beyond War Bonnet's short limits stood the agency building, its timeless sandstone a dull brown in the unrelenting sun. It was also a reminder of the day's business. His gait became slower as he crossed to the other side and returned toward the hotel.

Some distance along the hard-packed stretch near the hotel, in front of Leech's Hardware, a team waited, heads down. High on the wagon seat a woman held her child.

Terrell paid scant attention. Not long afterward he saw a man leave the store and go to the wagon, sunlight glinting on the blade of a long-handled axe he carried. The man stood talking to the woman, his back turned.

Then, as he approached closer, something sawed at

Terrell's nerves. His eyes raked the spare shape standing beside the wagon. He felt a stab of anger as he recognized Gibb Shepherd. Involuntarily he hauled up and hesitated. But it was too late to turn back, because the woman spoke a low warning.

Shepherd wheeled swiftly. Terrell met the stare. Their glances locked, but neither man spoke. Shepherd's mouth thinned. Walking casually, Terrell drew even with the wagon.

All at once Shepherd's voice erupted, flat and hating. "Wait a minute, Kinder!"

Terrell turned reluctantly.

"Gibb!" the woman said sharply. "Shut up!"

Sun had wrinkled and weathered her still young face, making her seem far older than her years. She sat holding a child. In sickening perception, Terrell saw fear whiten her cheeks. Her arms circled the child protectingly.

"I've stayed quiet long enough," her husband answered, not turning his head toward her.

"Gibb, you listen to me!"

Instead, Gibb Shepherd ignored her and clenched the axe handle in both bony hands. He stood stiff as a post, his face looking pinched, embittered, the skin taut as stretched rawhide over the prominent cheek bones.

His thinness shocked Terrell. Only the eyes were alive; in them shone a wild light. "I want no trouble with you," said Terrell. "Go on about your business."

"You rob a man and say that!" Shepherd started a slow advance.

The woman stiffened. "Gibb! Come back!"

Her husband kept coming slowly.

"Anybody can bid for that lease," snapped Terrell. "You know that."

"Nobody but you'd steal a man's living!"

At once, Terrell saw his mistake. There was no reasoning with Shepherd. "Go back to your wagon," he ordered curtly, and turned to leave.

"Don't tell me what to do!" Shepherd came on, deliberate, unswerving, his knuckles like white knobs on the axe.

Terrell froze. His right hand dropped instinctively to his holster.

"Gibb!" the woman cried. "He'll kill you!"

Again Shepherd seemed not to hear, and the fear in the woman's warning shook Terrell. For once in his life he acted uncertainly in the face of violence.

He stepped backward a pace and said: "Damn you, man, show some sense."

Shepherd's eyes blazed. He advanced to the walk's edge and halted. "You've gone too far," he muttered in a dead voice.

Terrell felt his tolerance crack. "Stop right there!" he ordered. "I'll have no Jayhawk cow thief. . . ."

There wasn't time to finish. With a shout, Gibb Shepherd leaped to the walk and swung the axe. The woman screamed. Terrell dodged just as the blade cut a shining arc past his face. For a tick of time Shepherd was thrown off balance by his own savagery, his guard down. But Terrell stood locked in a curious paralysis, rooted, incapable of movement.

Even as he stayed frozen, Shepherd two-handed the axe up once more, swiftly, a killing gleam in his eyes. Then, on instinct, Terrell back-stepped and bumped into the store's door frame. He saw the blur of the striking blade, and jumped sideways as Shepherd rushed in. The heavy steel thudded into the door siding, whacking deep, buried there. Shepherd tore at the handle.

At last Terrell moved forward. Before Shepherd could rip the handle free, he took one leaping stride, his knotted hands rising. He crashed his big fist to the long jaw. He saw Shepherd fall heavily upon the walk.

For a full moment Shepherd lay stunned. Then, slowly, his arms and legs stirred. He got an elbow under him, but he could not rise. Standing over him, legs braced, Terrell just now realized that he'd made no effort to use his pistol, and wondered why. He saw puzzlement break across the pale eyes and heard his own voice speaking in an odd tone.

"Your family's waiting."

Shepherd just stared.

Without thought, Terrell turned and strode rapidly across the street, past the wagon where the woman sat hushed, all eyes, her child held to her. He walked straight to the nearest store front, a saddle shop. Inside, he pulled up short and gazed around without seeing, breathing hard. He discovered that he was trembling, and yet he felt relieved of a tremendous load.

The white head of the old saddle maker bobbed into his vision, out of the shop's gloom. A voice he knew said: "Shepherd was asking for it if a man ever was. But you didn't shoot."

Terrell, not answering, turned to face the street. He saw Gibb Shepherd lay the axe in the wagon bed and climb stiffly to the seat, ignoring the stares of the small crowd outside the hardware store and the Cattle King. Speaking to the team, Shepherd reined off toward the agency. He drove slackly, without interest, his thin shoulders humped.

Within a matter of moments the crowd broke up. Terrell saw the images as blurs, no single face standing out at first. Now some of these people began drifting in the agency's direction. Among them he recognized Colonel DeWitt Richmond, straight and angular.

An inertia gripped Terrell, and he did not understand

himself. He had no idea how long he stood in the saddle shop before he saw Bert McGrath come heavily up the street, a small packet of papers in his hand.

His eyes followed McGrath as he paced out of sight. Afterward, he asked the saddle maker sharply: "What time is it, Jim?"

"Quarter to three. Lease sale's three o'clock, isn't it?"

Terrell nodded, already going out the door. His boots tapped the walk, and he turned—away from the agency, heading for Joel Creed's livery. He wouldn't wait for McGrath or old Fargo.

Although striding slowly, he had the feeling of running. The realization angered him unreasonably, pricked at his pride. Hadn't he told Buell and McGrath he wouldn't attend the bidding? True. Certainly there was no question of fear involved.

It wasn't clear to him just when, or how, he began to notice the change in War Bonnet—its somber stillness. It seemed that the town, drowsing in the sweltering afternoon heat, waited for something. Unexpectedly old danger signals beat inside him. He paused in stride and glanced over his shoulder. The street was almost empty, save for a man entering the hotel. He felt a little foolish. *What's got into me?* he thought, and brushed the unease away and went on. He'd simply lived too many years under the old set of rules, when primitive instincts of warning often meant survival.

He passed the wagon yard and saw the high frame of the stables. Nobody lounged out front, which wasn't unusual for this hour of the day. Neither did he see Creed in the runway.

Creed's cramped office faced open in greeting. Terrell walked toward it and found it empty. There was no use waiting for Creed, who kept his own hours, so Terrell placed money on the desk and returned to the runway. His gelding was in the usual stall, near the barn's center.

He turned to get his horse. After no more than a few paces, he perceived a change in the building—the rear doors were closed, leaving the barn dark. Slipshod as Creed was, he seldom. . . .

Something crackled within Terrell, the old warnings drumming, and this time he did not disregard them. He lunged low for a darkened stall, drawing his pistol in the same burst of motion. But before he'd gone two racing steps, he saw the flash of flame and felt one leg buckle like rotten wood. He fell and rolled, hearing the deafening roar of the gun and the banging of the terrified horses on the stall boards.

He still had his pistol, and he fired at the tall shadow making the spitting flashes—fired till the hammer clicked empty, the pinpoint of flame vanished, and he thought he heard a body fall.

And then, as if delayed, a bullet whanged close. Quickly another gun joined in, the two shots jamming together. Afterward the barn fell as still as ever, except for the horses.

A blackness dropped over Terrell Kinder, a growing blanket that came fast. He tried to drag himself up on the sound knee. For the first time his strong body did not respond to his driving will. He collapsed suddenly, felt straw litter under his face.

He heard boots. Hands lifted and turned him gently, and old Fargo's face took focus in the gloom. "Terrell!" he burst out. "Look at me, boy!" There came distant steps and vague faces, and old Fargo's voice seemed to fade and then to climb. "You fools! Don't stand there! Get the doctor!"

Terrell remembered being carried into the office, and even there, upon the bunk, the darkness followed. Nausea rolled within him. He could feel the blood running down his thigh.

He didn't know when she came in, but suddenly Leigh

Richmond was near. She hovered over him and seized his hand and kept saying his name, over and over.

He said: "It's too late to stop McGrath. Get word to Shepherd, tell him he can sub-lease from me."

She made a tiny crying sound. "Father went to offer him a job. Oh, Terrell, it's all right!"

"Leigh, what answer did you give to that other man's proposal?"

Men, tramping noisily into the office, cut across his words.

Somebody said: "Ennis Buell is back there with Nels Ivy, both dead. Remember Ivy?"

Leigh Richmond's face was so near that he caught the scent of her hair. "There's your answer, Terrell. Buell tried to kill you when I told him I wouldn't marry him."

"Buell!" The scene this morning came back to Terrell— Ennis Buell coming by the ranch, making certain Terrell came to town. But Nels Ivy!

Old Fargo said heavily: "You got Ivy. Buell was my meat. Ivy'd just finished serving his time and come back. Buell must've hired him." Fargo loomed over Terrell, gaunt and apologetic. "I spotted Ivy, followed him here. He came early, then Buell slipped in, and it put me between them. I couldn't see Ivy good, and he shot before I could. . . ." His voice shaded off, miserable and self-damning.

"Much obliged anyway, Fargo. You've always been my right-hand man."

Old Fargo scrubbed a thorny hand across his eyes and faced away abruptly. It was, Terrell knew suddenly, a long overdue acknowledgment to a loyal man.

"I've been pretty rough," he said aloud to both Leigh and Fargo. "Hard to change a man, I guess."

"I was wrong, too," he heard her answer. "Terrell, I was

watching from my room. I saw you and Shepherd. You had every excuse to kill him. Why, I'm just beginning to understand you."

"Know what I was thinking, Leigh, as I went down? That big house . . . all empty. Nobody in it."

"But there will be. You know that now," Leigh said softly.

She held on to him, fiercely, while he fought back the crowding blackness. He stirred, trying to speak again, but Leigh touched her fingers to his lips. "Be quiet, Terrell. Everything's going to be all right now."

Be Brave, My Son

In the smoldering heat of the railroad coach, Horse breathed smoke and cinders. Beyond the window the white man's strange world was passing. He watched with faraway eyes, thinking of graceful brown hawks sailing across a bright sky and of blue-hazed mountains rising above sweeping folds of fragrant prairie.

He turned. The guard was tramping down the aisle, scrutinizing each Indian and making marks in his black book. He did this each time after the train stopped in one of the white man's numerous big villages, puzzling places that could not be moved swiftly out of danger like a sensible teepee.

Horse, knowing what to expect, let his handcuffed hands go lax. He showed an expressionless face as the guard, lurching up, muttered the word "boy," marked in the book, and went on.

Horse straightened. Although he had lived only seventeen summers, hadn't he, alone, brought back many ponies from the stone corral by the soldiers' house at Medicine Bluff? For that he was now a captive with his warring Comanche tribesmen, and some Kiowas, Cheyennes, and Arapahoes. The old warriors said the soldiers were taking them to prison in the "hot country" far to the southeast, to a place they had never been. Likely they would never see their prairie homes again. Only this morning they had passed through the largest village seen thus far, then crossed a broad and powerful river, terrifying in size to a Plains Indian. Every snort of the belching iron monster, Horse realized, was taking him farther away.

He rose and moved down the aisle, searching the dejected faces for encouragement. No one looked up until he came to Mamanti—Sky Walker, the Kiowa chief and medicine man, once a great man. The fierce, glittering eyes bored into Horse's somber face and away, that was all.

When Horse returned to his seat, he became quite still. Once more the thought drummed. The iron things holding him like a mule had been made for a white man's thick wrists, not the slender bones of a young Comanche.

Deep dusk hazed the unfamiliar land when the train pulled off on a sidetrack and waited, engine chuffing. Horse could see a single lantern bobbing ahead. In the coach's mealy gloom the coppery, high-boned warrior faces were almost invisible. A homesick old Kiowa was chanting: *Hi-yah, hi-yah, he-yah.*

Beside him, Horse heard a shuffle of movement. Sky Walker stood there. Unexpectedly his manacled hands rose, as if in prayer, and touched Horse's shoulder, pressing. He said—"Be brave, my son."—and turned away, gone.

He knows, Horse thought.

A moment later he was startled as another iron horse burst roaring from the opposite direction. *Now,* he thought suddenly, *when the soldiers will not hear.* He stood, his bleeding wrists swinging free. But all his resolve fled at the thought of leaving his friends. He was trembling. And even as he hesitated, the other train rushed by and the coach fell still again.

It was the *hissing* of the engine and the forward jerking of the prisoners' car that roused him finally. Then, almost against his will, he drew his blanket in front of his lowered head and plunged through the glass window. A crashing din broke around him. He seemed to drop a long way before he felt the brutal impact of rocks.

For long moments he lay stunned, beside the tracks. Faintly, yet growing stronger, he could hear soldiers shouting and the screech of the halting train. Boots were pounding on the roadbed when he pushed himself up and ran reeling into the darkness.

Not until he was panting within a thicket did he understand that he was actually free. Later, when the lanterns disappeared and the train chugged on, he turned his face toward the west, following the trail of the iron road.

At daylight he slumped down and gulped the water of a shallow creek, bathed his raw wrists, and lay back, used up. His long idleness as a prisoner had left his body soft. Rested, he ate sparingly from his bandanna pack of hard bread and bacon saved out of his rations and took stock of himself. Above all, he must be brave! And he must not be seen—a Comanche in fringed moccasins, breechclout, and fringed buckskin leggings which reached from foot to hip, with his parted black hair forming a braid on each side.

Lying there, he felt lost and bewildered. To make his way back to the plains where the prairie dogs barked, he must imitate his brother the coyote, hide by day and travel at night. To him, his escape now seemed more foolish than wise. He had little food and not even a knife, although couldn't he see the sky and feel the spring sun? New strength flowed into him.

Taking grass, he brushed out his tracks and crossed on flat rocks to the other side of the creek. Along the bank towered an ancient elm tree. Rushing floodwaters had mined its roots. After wiping out his footprints to the tree, he crawled under its base and curled up. Sleep clutched him.

★ ★ ★ ★ ★

Horse opened his eyes as suddenly as if someone had called his name. Blinking, he saw by the shadows that he had slept a long time. A clattering toward the iron road on the creek had awakened him. The unmistakable *clack* of shod hoofs upon rocks.

Peering out, he shrank back. Pony soldiers, yellow stripes down the sides of their breeches—soldiers led by a chief on a white horse—were crossing the creek in twos. Fear pushed over him. He watched them stringing out toward his hiding place, their eyes searching all about. So many soldiers he could feel the trembling of the earth.

Of a sudden, above and behind his den, he heard a rider halt and shout. Close to panic, he squirmed to make himself smaller. Next he glimpsed the braced forelegs of a white horse sliding down the bank. A black boot came into view. What could he do when the soldier dismounted and poked his gun under the tree?

Moments. Horse could hear much noise on the creek. That meant the soldiers were surrounding his tree. And then, in drenching relief, he saw the cavalry mount shake its bridle and dip its muzzle to drink, while the black boot of its rider stayed in the stirrup.

After they rode off, he had to will himself against scrambling out like a rabbit and fleeing the other way. In the stillness Horse dozed.

Before sundown he heard horses again, and he recognized the drumming racket of the cavalry column returning. To his dismay the pony soldiers camped behind his den. Their voices rang through the woods, and shortly the pungency of their fires and their food made his mouth juices run, and so again he locked his mind to patience.

The yellow eye of a hunter's moon was watching when

Horse ascended the sloping creekbank. Ravels of smoke still swam through the timber. Familiar sounds stirred, the good snuffle and stamp of horses. At once he was tempted to take one. Wasn't his formal name, He-Hunts-for-the-Horses, bestowed by a famous warrior and therefore a strong name? His excitement ebbed as quickly, cooled by a voice that said he was safer afoot.

He started drifting away, only to halt not many steps on, motionless, catching the scent of a white man's pipe. A sentry stood squarely across his path. Horse went cold, but did not move. He heard the man cough, shift his boots, and look toward the sleeping camp. Without a sound, Horse slipped forward. He could have touched the soldier's back when he passed. Onward, he heard the man turn about. There was no other sound. Lengthening his strides, he saw the iron road pointing west in the pale light.

Horse had to summon all his self-denial not to wolf his remaining rations the next day. When crossing the *Llano Estacado,* the Staked Plains, his elders had reminded him often as a child never to whimper when hungry or thirsty. He understood again. It was a Comanche's life to endure, to suffer. Even so, his little hoard of food did not last past the third day. He traveled far that night on the railroad ties and the flinty roadbed, pausing only when trains thundered out of the filmy darkness, a broad face, high-cheeked and proud, solemn with loneliness, turned to the fleeting lights. Twice he circled wide around villages to avoid dogs.

Dawn found him taking cover in tall grass, stumbling from weakness. Besides hunger, the moist, heavy air, unlike the accustomed dry heat of the high prairies, also took his strength. An awareness deepened. Unless he got food soon, he must give himself up or starve. Yet the thought of surrender was intolerable. Around him the insects droned a lulling chorus. He dozed.

Hunger shook him awake earlier than usual. This was not a safe hiding place. Daylight had caught him in open country, short of a patch of timber. He could see farmhouses. As he looked off there was a whirring, and a yellow grasshopper sprang and lay crackling at his feet. Horse trapped it on impulse. He started to let it go; instead, he hesitated, remembering. Many fat grasshoppers whirred in the grass. Thereafter he was busy capturing them and eating their hind legs for lunch. Later, hearing a cautious rustling under the dry litter, he uncovered a terrapin, a Comanche delicacy when roasted.

All at once Horse could bear his hunger no further, and he went crouching toward the woods. On the way he picked up a fragment of rock below the railroad embankment. It was flat and pointed. By afternoon he owned a crude knife, its split wooden handle wrapped in buckskin fringes, a slender hickory rod, shaved straight and smooth, a block of softer wood, a bird's nest, and a supply of twigs and branches. Behind a fallen tree he gathered everything and sat back to watch the sky change, forcing himself to wait.

Near darkness had come when he dropped on one knee and twirled the hickory shaft vertically into the block. He was performing the old Comanche fire-making method, in use before Mexican traders had brought flint and steel to his people. He was unskilled. His palms burned. Nothing happened. Moving the rod nearer the edge, he drilled another hole and from it cut a narrow opening. He spun the stick furiously, until his hands felt on fire.

Like a signal a puff of smoke climbed out of the bird's nest around the fire cavity. He coaxed, blowing gently; the nest caught, flared. He put on twigs and sticks, and, as the small scarlet cone leaped higher, it was as though it were life itself, as if he could see the campfires of his people. He roasted the terrapin, his cooking fire masked before the log, and afterward he saved the shell for a drinking cup.

For two days Horse stayed in the friendly woods, resting and slyly hunting terrapins, hunting cottontails with a club, killing black snakes, and after dark smoke-drying the extra meat for his long journey. His little patch of woods was like an island floating on a green sea of pasture and meadow. He rejected the brown haystack's comfort on the west side, preferring the timber.

He jerked alert early the following morning, astonished to hear a blaring which had last sounded in his ears near the pony soldiers' fort by the spirit bluff—the clear notes of a bugle.

He stared, a trapped feeling upon him. The chief on the white horse was halting his men in the pasture east of the woods. Hardly had the bugle ceased blowing when more troopers crossed the tracks and joined the others.

Horse began throwing his possessions into the blanket and brushing out camp signs, fearful that his sudden movements might be noticed. Running west, he saw no place to hide except the brown haystack. He raced for it, and then an instinct stronger than reason sent him toward a grassy draw. Flattening down, he looked back. His strength seemed to leave him.

Soldiers were scouting through the woods. Out they came and straight ahead, toward the draw, until they noted the haystack. Veering across to it, they commenced pulling and poking. There was considerable milling and gesturing. Afterward the soldiers' chief raised his arm; they bunched and fled westward along the tracks.

Another fear settled over Horse while he watched, and a

sensation of shame. Instead of going on, of enduring, he had stopped to fill his stomach. Thus the soldiers rode between him and the awesome river. He had no choice but to follow at a distance.

That evening he circled the soldiers' winking fires and, returning to the iron road, swung into his long-striding trot.

Many times the sun went down before Horse approached the great river. He glimpsed it under the sinking rays of a fading day, writhing by like an enormous muddy-brown snake. And again he knew his Plains Indian's misgivings of its frightening power, its terrible strangeness. A thick pall of smoke hung above the vast village on the other side which he remembered hearing the prison train guards call St. Louis.

He had expected to cross the river simply by following the iron horse's trail on its high, spidery legs. But as he scouted closer, his anticipation vanished. Soldiers guarded the place where the trail started over the water; even now they were gazing his way. He crouched lower.

Dusk veiled the countryside. A slim shadow left the grass beyond the tracks. It paused, faced west. Then it dissolved among the tall stalks of a cornfield. Later, several miles below the bridge, while the moon swam by in the river, Horse made his bed in another cornfield. After a breakfast of raw corn and smoked rabbit, he trotted down to inspect the river, finding blackberries and green summer grapes as he went. Driftwood littered the willow-lined shore.

Ever since his escape he had dreaded facing the river. Up close, feeling its humid breath, hearing its violent passage, his uneasiness increased. And yet as the early sunlight touched the water with streaks of reddish gold and the mist curled off and a woods-scented breeze sprang up, he lost a portion of his fear. Enough so that he swam in the calm water by the shore.

It was then that he spied the raft, eight man-length logs lashed together. He towed it ashore. Searching the driftwood, he found a splintered plank for a paddle.

The sun had burned the sky clear when Horse placed his thin blanket pack aboard, shoved off, and took up the clumsy paddle. At first his progress was gradual and uneventful. Farther out he stroked. Yonder, he sighted the long black shape of a huge raft and, nearer, a steamboat churning up the middle, snarling smoke. People waved. Their excited voices carried to him as though they stood but a throw away.

As he stared back, a hidden force, wild and savage, seemed to seize his raft and hurl it downriver. He was rushing and gliding, shooting ahead, both fearful and elated. He kept paddling for the west side. Despite his efforts it looked as distant as before. Behind him the village vanished. He was swept faster. After a little he could make out a house in the woods and the glittery sheen of sunlight on leaves where cottonwoods laced a sandbar. He *was* closer. He hunched his shoulders, paddling faster.

He scarcely noticed a streak on the swift water. One twinkling it was ahead of him, and in no time, without warning, he was upon the black snag. He heard a ripping crash as the raft rose and flipped. After that he saw the muddy coils of the river reaching for him.

He seemed to struggle upward forever through murky darkness, toward an elusive and shifting light. He broke water suddenly, the river's roar pounding in his ears. He shook his head and spat water. Over there, misty green under the blazing sunlight, the cottonwoods beckoned from the sandbar. Exhausted, he finally made it.

Horse no longer followed the iron road. He watched the smoky sun, his swinging trot bearing southwest by instinct. Thin to emaciation, he had worn out his moccasins prior to reaching the big river, and his leggings hung as shreds down his lean thighs.

The land through which he passed was heavy with the drowse of summer, the season when his people would be listening to the bellowing *roo-roo-oo* of the buffalo bulls. Sometimes he found melons in the fields, roots in the woods. He gorged when he had meat and could use his new fire drill; when he had none, he fixed his mind to run ahead of him. The mighty river, which had taken all his possessions, had given him far more in return, fresh courage and the will to endure, for to a Comanche the greatest purpose in life was to be brave, always.

Sometimes he seemed to move in a grayish trance. Still, when hunger pains gnawed and bad dreams floated through his mind, the image of the great open sky and the sentinel mountains would return to him, the prairies below dark with buffalo, and upon awakening he would be brave again.

Horse hurried. Long ago he had traveled through the rough hills west of the river. A constant thought pressed. He must reach home before his strength gave out. His movements were shadow-like, his senses extra keen. He slept in snatches and had acquired a disdain for danger. Often he dared trot the lonely, dusty roads in daylight. If he heard a horseman or wagon coming, he would conceal himself and afterward stride on, as wise as brother coyote, knowing when to hide, when to stir.

So gradually did the face of the country change that Horse, in his dull weariness, wasn't aware of it for a while. There were fewer houses. The land was broadening. He traveled all of each day. But he was growing weaker. He had to rest more often. His once free-swinging trot was a ragged jog. His weakness made him a poor hunter. At times he discovered himself paused, head down, stupefied by exhaustion, weaving on bare feet, puzzled as to his direction until he looked up at the guiding sun.

A day began when he knew that, if he faltered even once and lay down, he could not rise again. He knew, for his spirit was beginning to wander from his punished body. Before his eyes blurred, undulating folds danced weirdly.

All morning he had been jogging head down; occasionally he reeled. His arms hung. A sound caused him to drag step. A barking. He stopped, his dull senses straining to respond. Again the barking, brisk, staccato. In a rush he recognized the scolding chirp of prairie dogs.

He lifted his head and gazed southwest, held motionless. Something darted there—swift, brown creatures wheeling and sailing back and forth across the clear sky. Beyond them, hooded by blue haze, loomed the dim humps of the mountains that he had begun to fear existed only in his vanishing dreams.

Horse's throat filled. He knelt in the warm prairie grass, made strong again.

The Town Killer

King Roebuck, square hands on hips, eyed his calf-branding crew with satisfaction. It was early morning, and the land still lay cool and fresh. Smoke from the post-oak fire whetted a man's appetite all over again, spread a tang on the high, thin air. A rider shook out his first loop.

"Ed?" King asked, looking around. "Where's Ed Pittman?"

Although his strong voice carried distinctly, nobody answered. Several men exchanged sheepish glances.

King kept at them. "Ed sick?"

Cap Strawn, the Anvil's foreman, looked up from his irons fire. "Ed, he didn't come in last night."

"Where'd he go?"

Strawn measured his cherry-red irons, rose, and sauntered across in his bowed, unhurried gait, seeming all bones and sharp angles and possessed of an infinite scorn for haste, yet always in the right place. Even after all these years, he was the same to King. A never-changing, sun-punished man with an astonishing energy in his spare frame, his blue eyes washed out, but serenely trapping a wisdom of men, animals, and country. He seldom spoke above an even tone; he did not now.

"Blanco . . . he rode into Blanco."

King stared hard, his throat swelling. "What the hell, Cap?

You know the orders. . . ." Too late, he caught himself, seeing the startled hurt build into the lined, gray-stubbled face.

"I know," Strawn said wearily. "No man rides into Blanco alone. Happens Ed just took off, like a boy will, and he's not the first around here to go nighthawking after some girl."

"You know how I feel about that town, Cap."

"Never tolerated it none myself." The wattles under-hanging Strawn's wrinkled neck suddenly quivered. "Know something, King? Seems I sort of remember back when somebody else used to spark a certain girl in Blanco. Maybe he ought to again. Might be good medicine." Having said his piece, Cap Strawn went deliberately back to his fire.

King, watching him, was filled with a grudging admiration he dared not show here. Only one man could backtalk him in that fashion and get away with it. He found himself searching for the mending words, words that he could not express.

"Cap," he said at last, "if Ed's not in by noon, send into town after him."

Walking off, King Roebuck wondered just where the morning had come apart on him. Here he was treating old Cap like an ordinary hired hand in front of the crew. And Cap, knowing King's tender spots as no other man did, had rubbed it in about Holly.

There was overdue ledger work awaiting him, and he made tracks for the ranch house. It stood two stories high, three-feet-thick brown stone walls scarred by both Comanches' and outlaws' bullets. A mute reminder of the Anvil's stormy past and of that of the first King Roebuck, who had died in brawling Blanco so long ago that now King thought of his father almost as a legendary figure instead of the dim, proud image in a small boy's memory.

Inside the house he felt the banked coolness around him. His boots beat vacantly in the silent dwelling as he tramped to his combination office and bedroom. He aimed his hat for the elkhorn rack across the room—and missed by a foot. He let the peaked hat stay on the floor, aware of a cankering rebellion whose exact source eluded him.

He was still standing, stiff-bodied, vaguely troubled, a high-shouldered man ridden down to the lean, and brown hair unruly above a face that was both strong and impatient, when horse sound reached him. King cocked his head. The racket came on, growing louder, a drumfire of hurry. All at once he left the room.

Standing on the porch, he saw Phil Overstreet, his legal representative from town, bring a hard-used gelding into the flinty yard and dismount. Despite his dusty ride, his smartly cut dark suit and white shirt still looked fresh. His black riding boots shone with a polished brilliance. He faced about, revealing muscular shoulders that sloped to a slim waist. He was quick of movement, poised and confident, a man in his early thirties, some years the senior of King. Strolling forward, he had a latent swagger, as if endowed by special license to go wherever he chose—a mere mannerism, and part and parcel of this ambitious, driving man who so competently handled the ranch's affairs, yet King sensed an obscure feeling of intrusion. He forced it aside to greet Overstreet warmly.

"How's Holly these days?"

"Well, I'm sure."

"You're the lucky cuss, Phil. Sometimes I wonder if you really realize it."

A frown crossed Overstreet's smooth, well-made face. "King, I didn't come here to discuss Holly. I've got bad news."

"Any time a man rides hard from Blanco. . . . Well, let me have it."

"It's Ed Pittman . . . he's dead."

"No!"

"True. He was found this morning in an alley . . . shot, murdered. Must have happened last night late, because he was seen earlier. I rode out as soon as I heard."

King bowed his head, too stunned to speak. Ed Pittman had been a dependable hand. Obliging and popular, clean-cut, the sort of young rider everybody liked. King had given him his first job several years ago, and Ed had stuck, proving himself more than once. Now the undeniable loyalty due a good man demanded that something must be done.

A great tide of anger swamping him, King jerked to start for the corrals.

"Don't dash off half-cocked," Overstreet cautioned.

"I'm not. We'll go in for Ed's body. He has no folks, so we'll bury him in the ranch cemetery. Give him a decent resting place with my folks."

"After that?"

King smashed his right fist into his palm. "Then there will be a reckoning in Blanco. We're not going to take this."

"Hold on. I know Blanco's been a sore spot with you over the years. Certainly and rightfully for personal reasons. But violence won't work these days, King. Times have changed from when a man could ride into a town and tear it down."

King sneered. "They murdered Ed there, didn't they? And I won't ask you if anybody's been arrested yet, because I know there hasn't been. There's nothing but slipshod law in Blanco . . . you know that. And you say gun play won't work! Which is where you're wrong, Phil. That's the one thing they do savvy in Blanco."

"Better way," said Overstreet, pursing his lips.

"You mean the right-of-way?"

Overstreet drew out a linen handkerchief and set about

dusting his boots. The gesture struck King not only as unnecessary, but loaded with deliberate meaning, although Overstreet had always leaned toward flourish.

"Exactly," the lawyer went on, "and the railroad's interested. You see, Southwestern doesn't want to go through Blanco if it can help it. Even with free easement, which Blanco's businessmen haven't offered, it would be pretty costly laying track and building bridges across up-and-down country. . . . You, King, own the only other feasible route. That's across your south range. Rather, one corner of it."

"I'm aware of that."

"But do you see what it means?" Overstreet exclaimed, his pale face flushed. "The power it gives you!"

"We can talk about it later."

"If Southwestern goes around," Overstreet persisted, "Blanco ends up withered on the vine . . . like this." He knotted his hand, the fingers as sensitive as a woman's, squeezing until his knuckles whitened. "New towns will spring up along the tracks. Blanco will soon lose the county seat."

"Later," King answered, annoyed at being delayed.

"Say the word, and I'll start drawing up easement papers. I can promise you a good price. How about six o'clock in my office?"

"All right," King gave in, and was gone for the corrals, calling Cap Strawn.

In the hanging heat of late afternoon King Roebuck and his armed Anvil crew, followed by the ranch wagon, came down from the surrounding rocky hills into Blanco's unkempt outskirts. At the first alley, Overstreet pulled up.

"Six o'clock, then . . . my office," he reminded, and rode off briskly.

King followed him with his eyes, understanding why a local man might wish to avoid lining up with the Anvil in public today. At the same time he could not but feel disappointment, for to him loyalty wasn't a trifle to be removed at will, worn only down side streets.

He rounded a corner onto Main Street, and there, before him, lay the gray, dust-powdered heart of Blanco. Ox carts and overland freighters, plus a sweet spring, had begun a town bright with promise, a promise never fulfilled. As long as King could remember, Blanco had reminded him of a shiftless old renegade, uncombed and unwashed, never to be trusted, and crouching beneath the hills. There had been a time when he had ridden here to see Holly, but never to trade.

Down the street he could see men gathering around the undertaking parlor, men gawking, staring as the Anvil moved in unafraid. *Let 'em wonder,* King thought, and found himself keyed tight for trouble, eager for it.

His scornful gaze fixing them, the Anvil owner rode in close and swung down. His crew pressed in behind him, with Cap Strawn at his shoulder, he entered the undertaker's, dreading what he'd soon see.

He studied the waxen young face on the plank table for a lengthy, helpless, fury-killing time. Then, without warning, he squared on the undertaker, who kept clasping and unclasping his bony hands.

"Where was he shot?" King asked.

"In . . . in the back."

King eyed Strawn. "I knew it!" He turned back to the undertaker. "How many times?"

"Three . . . four, it was."

In quiet outrage, King Roebuck said: "Put him in the wagon, Cap. Take Ed home."

As hatless cowboys clumped in and out of the room, King

93

went to the boardwalk under the gallery. The crowd outside, curious and murmuring, had strayed back. Through it now a townsman named Ross Murdine made a path to Roebuck.

"Howdy, King. Sorry it was one of your boys."

King drew in against the friendly tone of Murdine's resonant voice. Murdine was a man of middle years, running to tallow, and, although his manner was that of an easy-to-meet storekeeper, there was neither awe of the Anvil nor fear of the spread about him. He held out his hand.

King stared at it. Then his chin came up. He made no motion.

Murdine recoiled, heat flushing his face. "You're not blaming *me?*"

King shook his head. "Not you, in particular. Except you're part of Blanco. Your town's rotten to the core and no mealy-mouthed words can make up for a murdered boy. I want that understood."

Dimly King realized that the crowd had stilled, that every face seemed turned his way. Murdine hadn't moved.

Boots scuffed. Cap Strawn, his grizzled head uncovered, slowly left the building. He was followed by four solemn-faced Anvil men, bearing a yellow-new coffin. They reached the wagon, grunted, and lifted and slid, then moved stiffly to their horses.

"I realize this is an awkward time to talk," Murdine said, low and careful. "And I know how the Anvil feels. Just don't blame the entire town for one killer's dirty work."

"But your town's going to pay."

"Pay? How . . . how do you mean?"

King heard himself answer without even thinking. "The railroad. Southwestern. I'm making my land available to them for a right-of-way."

"You'd do that? Break us?"

"I will."

"For a price, no doubt."

"A fair price," King corrected. "A fair price for my land."

"Well, let me tell you something," Murdine replied, turning for the crowd's benefit, his voice rising. "You'll have to move fast. Blanco's merchants just voted a free right-of-way through town. Tie that!"

For a brief moment King was caught off guard. But his temper came through, and he cried: "Then I'll give mine free! Flat prairie for your humped-up hills! I'll kill the town that killed Ed Pittman! You'll wither on the vine. . . ." Even as he spoke, it occurred to him that what he was saying weren't his words, but Overstreet's, and he had a sudden distaste for himself.

Murdine was shocked. "We . . . we won't let you ruin us!" he got out finally. "We'll find some way to stop you. You'll see."

He flung away, striding rapidly. The crowd gave ground.

Quitting the walk, King went across to where Strawn sat his horse apart from the crew, as if better to gauge the tempers around him.

"Clear 'em out, Cap."

"Suits me. I don't like the way this is buildin' up." The foreman lifted reins, only to drop his hand. A troubled look touched his eroded features. "You coming?"

"Not now. I'm due to meet Phil at six o'clock, close this deal once and for all. I'll bring a preacher out in the morning for Ed's funeral."

"Let me send some of the bunch on. Rest of us can sorter hang around." Strawn winked solemnly. "In case."

"And invite more trouble? No, Cap. I don't want a single

Anvil man left in Blanco. You understand?"

"That include me?"

"Cap, you heard me."

"But you aim to stay?"

Roebuck just eyed him.

"You're asking for it," Strawn warned in his placid way.

"Murdine won't try anything."

"I'm not so sure. Even a cottontail will bite if you take his living out of his mouth. If not Murdine, there's plenty of others who stand to be hurt if you kill this town." He lowered his voice. "King, you have to go that far?"

"You're against me?"

Strawn shifted uncomfortably. He took a deep breath, his straight on stare never lifting. "King," he said, "I used to figure I did a good job on you. Now I don't know. Maybe all I did was bring up a proud, hot-headed young pup so he could get his lamp blowed out. Amen."

He set his spurs, calling to the crew, and the Anvil formed in escort around the wagon and started off, a set rancor fixing the sun-burned faces.

King mounted, rode to the street's end, and stabled his gelding in the livery barn next to the wagon yard.

Angling back toward the hotel, he was conscious of an utter desolation. The Anvil was not popular here. Nobody spoke to him, and he recognized but few townsmen, a reminder of how little he'd really seen of Blanco and its people in recent years, except for Holly Winslow and Phil Overstreet.

Deep in thought as he went inside the Brazos Hotel, he brought up sharply as a voice said carefully: "King. Thought you'd come here to wait."

Roebuck wheeled instinctively and felt foolish instantly when he saw Overstreet. Otherwise, the lobby was empty. He said: "It's all right to play it safe, Phil, but don't come up on my blind side."

Overstreet grinned and strolled up. "Let's just say I'm being discreet. Blanco might not understand. . . . Listen, I was in the crowd. I heard Murdine threaten you. Watch him, King! Watch him as you've never watched any man before."

"You come here just to tell me that?"

"To warn you, King. I'm glad you're armed."

A quick exasperation filled King. "I don't believe Murdine would kill a man."

"You don't know him. I do." Overstreet gazed around, said—"See you about dark."—and was gone.

Presently, the desk clerk appeared, and King took a room. Instead of going upstairs, however, he returned to the lobby window to watch the street, restless, impatient of delay. The lobby clock said five. With time a weight upon him, he thought of Holly.

Hardly had the impulse struck than he was in motion. He forgot about Murdine, forgot Blanco as he saw the small, painted sign swaying over the shop front. There were dresses and hats in the window.

He entered with some doubt, half expecting to find Overstreet there.

Only Holly was there at this late hour, though, turning to him with a swift expression of surprise. His impression of her, he discovered, had not changed. It was a quickening current of feeling, as powerful and deep running as of old. She was a tall young woman, her hair dark and lustrous, her face rounded, her mouth full and sensitive. Her large eyes, of that shade of brown that is closest to smokiness, considered him pleasantly.

Why, she's glad to see me, he thought.

She held a light shawl, which she laid aside. "I was just

going out to look for you," she said airily.

"Blanco's a small place."

She gestured him to a chair and sat down herself. He sat there, wondering what her errand could have been, and sensing the strangeness of coming back. Once he'd paid regular calls in the cheerful parlor beyond, that spoke of Holly everywhere—in the flowered paper on the walls, the lace curtains, the hand-painted lamps.

She said in the same breath, becoming frank: "Bad news travels fast. By now everyone in town knows what you're going to do."

"Do they know what Murdine will do as well?" he inquired. "Will he try to get me?"

"Would that surprise you?"

"Guess not. I might do the same under similar circumstances." His voice roughened. "But there's right on my side, Holly. Ed Pittman was a good man. My friend. Blanco murdered him. I can't let that pass. I'd be no man if I did."

She clasped her hands in her lap, studying him a reasonable moment. "I understand the marshal is investigating."

"Aw, you talk like Murdine."

"Fair talk, I think. Only one person shot Ed Pittman. Certainly all Blanco is not responsible."

He said doggedly, bitterly: "This isn't the first time the Anvil's lost a good man in Blanco."

"I've heard the story." Understanding turned her expression gentle, and he saw a sweet-lipped gravity. "Your father died out there . . . in that street. A man shot him in the back and rode out of town."

"Twenty years ago," King muttered with feeling. "Cap Strawn had to hunt him down . . . he evened the score. Law here is no better now than it was then. Worse, maybe. We don't even know Ed's killer. We did know who killed my father."

She leaned forward, bringing a mingled regret and earnestness to bear upon him. "I'm sorry for what's happened . . . for poor Ed. But, King, does this feud between the Anvil and Blanco have to go on forever?"

"As long as I live," he answered at once. He stood up, his mouth compressing, and realized he was avoiding her eyes.

"Even if you found Ed's killer?"

"That wouldn't bring Ed back to life."

She made a small, helpless gesture. "King, tell me something. Why did you come here today?"

"Habit, I guess." It was odd, but he felt like smiling. "Because I used to come. You're the main reason I ever came to Blanco."

Color shot into her cheeks. She rose suddenly. "Why did you stop calling?"

"My welcome got a little thin, didn't it?"

"Did I tell you so?"

He considered her, deeply disturbed, understanding neither her nor himself at this moment. "You preferred Phil's company," he said flatly. "I thought it was pretty plain how. . . ."

"You thought. Perhaps your pride wouldn't let you find out."

A galling heat hit his face. "I won't hold any man's stirrup. You ought to know that by now." He was moving without thought, until he looked down into the liquid of her eyes. So close that he brushed her. His longing to take her in his arms was a steady, hammering force.

Holly stood very still. Something lived behind the dark eyes for an instant, then it passed, and King stepped back.

"I think I know you," she said, and there was a trace of pity in her voice that angered him. "You haven't changed. I guess you can't. Why, for years you've hauled supplies from Mesa . . . miles out of your way . . . rather than trade in Blanco. As a point of Roebuck honor." She was breathing deeply. "It's not good for you to hate for so long and so hard . . . something's happening to you. You'll make the whole town pay. People who've lived here all their lives, all these years, and never once harmed you or the Anvil."

"This why you were going to look me up?" he asked, deliberately cutting her short. "Just to tell me off?"

A quiet despair dragged into her tone. "I don't want you to do anything you'll be sorry for later."

"I won't . . . believe me . . . except for your business. To make up for that, I'll move you to the new county seat. Whatever you lose in the meantime, I'll make up. I'm sorry about that . . . nothing else."

"You needn't feel that way."

"Why not? I. . . ." He broke off as something warned him.

"Phil," she answered, looking slim and cool as she told him, "asked me to marry him."

He had expected this for several months, often speculating about what could have delayed the marriage. Yet now, learning of it, he still wasn't prepared.

He said: "I keep telling Phil he's a lucky man, and I hope you're happy." He went to the door.

"King, be careful. I wish you wouldn't sign that easement."

"I've given my word, Holly." His back was turned as he spoke. "Phil has the papers ready. Now . . . at his office." *And that,* he thought darkly, *is how it's going to be.*

He hurried outside into the purple dusk, surprised at how time had slipped away. As he turned up the dimming street, he had a new and terrible knowledge of loneliness.

Little by little it came to him that he was only half alert to his surroundings—a laxness, he knew ruefully, Cap Strawn could never excuse. He stopped and took stock.

Now and then a man hurried into the thickening twilight, for it was suppertime, the town passive, like a fallow field. Wind from the hills flung a pattering of grit against the plank walk, drummed the murky store windows. Beyond, in the last block, was Phil Overstreet's office down from the livery barn and wagon yard.

Approaching the hotel, King saw a man leave the lobby and station himself in front. It was Murdine, his manner stiff and troubled. He said: "Was hoping you'd change your mind."

"Then you don't know me," King said, pausing, catching the bulge of Murdine's coat around his hip. "I have not."

"I see." Murdine chewed his lower lip. He was not a begging man, and King knew he'd not ask again. As if resigned, Murdine dropped his arms suddenly and stepped backward. A motion that could mean anything.

"Well . . . ," King challenged, half around.

"Walk on."

"And show you my back?"

Disgust worked along Murdine's heavy mouth. "Listen, you're target for any one of a dozen men tonight. If it will make you feel any easier, though. . . ." He opened the screen door wide, in exaggeration, and entered, to stand once more by the lobby window.

King felt his temper pull tight, like a frayed rope. He had it under control by the time he reached the last side street. And it was then, glancing across, that he spotted movement in a doorway.

A thready excitement traveled through him as he froze. He put his back to a store wall and played his gaze across, up, and down the street. The man in the doorway hadn't stirred. Murdine, King saw, had come outside the hotel again. Finally, when the man across showed no signs of coming out, King began a slow, head-turning walk that brought him across the street and along the block to the adobe building he sought. He turned in and down a hall.

Overstreet's face looked flushed, under the lamplight. He was at his desk, coatless, his sleeves rolled to the elbows and his white shirt open at the collar, showing his strong neck column.

King's grin was wry. "Looks like you've had a day."

"I have." Overstreet reached for a tallish whisky decanter. "A drink?"

"Not tonight."

"As you say, it's been a shrew of a day." Overstreet poured quickly and long, raised his glass. "Here's to Southwestern and Anvil."

King nodded without enthusiasm. Overstreet had his drink, lifted a sheet of paper covered in his slanting handwriting. "The deed, King. Read and sign."

King settled himself. He read through it once, twice, nodded in approval, picked up Overstreet's pen, and dipped into the glass inkwell. At the last moment he hesitated.

"I leave out something?" Overstreet asked.

"Reads all right. No, something Holly said just came to me."

"Holly?"

King had to grin at the concern he saw. "It was just a friendly visit, believe me."

Overstreet bent toward Roebuck. "Of course," he said, although sounding touchy. "What did she say?"

"Plenty about my right-of-way. She's against letting the railroad through."

Overstreet eased back in his chair. "Naturally."

"She mentioned, too," King said, "that you had finally popped the big question."

"That all?" Overstreet asked, coming slowly erect.

"Isn't that enough? Man, what do you want . . . the moon?"

Decisively King dipped the pen again and held it motionless over the paper, thinking: *I've put it off long enough.* His mouth firmed. He signed his name in an angular hand, passed the deed across, and said: "You can get in touch with Southwestern. And mind recording it for me at the courthouse?"

"First thing in the morning, King." Overstreet placed the single sheet inside an envelope and, reaching for his coat on a chair, slipped the envelope to an inner pocket, saying: "This way I won't forget."

"One more favor, Phil. Be obliged if you'll make arrangements for a preacher to come out in the morning. Ed's funeral. I've decided to go back tonight."

"Glad to." Overstreet sat relaxed, his muscular shoulders loose. "Where's your horse, King?"

"Stabled. End of the street."

"In that case keep an eye out behind you . . . toward town. If you like, I'll go along to the livery barn with you."

"Never mind. Thanks." Glancing back from the door, King noted Overstreet still at his desk. "Going to work all night, Phil?"

"Few odds and ends to clean up. . . . Good night, King. I'll take care of everything."

Well, that finishes it, King thought. Going out, he noticed the hallway opening on the alley and, briefly, it tempted him. His walk was paced, thoughtful, and depression seemed to catch up with him as he neared the black mouth of the street entrance. The feeling that rode him hard made him halt, wondering why he felt no satisfaction for what he'd just done. Stopped dead, the murmur of the street reaching him for the first time, he realized suddenly that in his preoccupation he'd almost blundered through the doorway.

In vast self-disgust he eased along the wall to the door. For long moments he observed the outside gloom until his eyes adjusted, then he stepped to the wall. He moved two strides and hauled around, his glance sweeping the early darkness behind and across from him.

There was no nearby movement. Men loafed around the hotel and saloons, but King couldn't make out Murdine among them. Again he sifted the shadows. At last, assured, he launched a measured walk, deciding: *Murdine missed his chance when I came out.*

It wasn't long before he stopped, seeing the cluttered wagon yard on his right. Beyond, bulking high against the skyline, rose the horse barn. Again he searched behind him, half turned.

When he first felt it, he never knew because it came so gradually—a sensation of wrongness, a brush of sound he felt rather than heard.

Then with startling suddenness, he heard: "King! The wagon yard!"

He wheeled at a crouch, dragging up his pistol, facing into a dimness cut by bright stabbings. Something hot struck his side. He felt himself going down, his ears aroar. But even as he dropped, instinctively he was rolling. He had to move fast, and he kept rolling and twisting and came up beside a wagon wheel. For an instant he lost all movement. Then, in the wild dark, he glimpsed a white blur. It evolved into a figure darting at him from around the far end of the wagon.

A bullet *whined,* and King thrust his gun toward the white

glob, firing and firing. Not ceasing until the man cried out, broke stumbling away. King heard him fall.

Afterward, all King caught was the rush of boots. It registered on him curiously that he couldn't stand, even though he gripped wagon spokes. Nausea swamped him. And an old man's savage face—Cap Strawn's, it was—loomed over him. King could feel rough hands seize his shoulders.

"King! Speak up!"

"Yeah, Cap." His voice sounded dull, far away. "He's over yonder."

"Shut up! You're hurt!"

"Past that wagon, Cap. Go see."

Instead, Strawn called out into the darkness, which all of a sudden was filled with running men.

"Lend a hand here!" Strawn bawled. "Get him down to Holly Winslow's!"

Swinging lantern light rose and fell, throwing a yellowish, unreal glare. And somewhere an incredulous voice shouted: "It's Phil Overstreet . . . stone dead!"

There were muffled voices. King Roebuck opened his eyes. By degrees his gaze focused on pink flowers, an entire wall of them. Then he knew, even before he moved his eyes. He was in Holly Winslow's parlor, and before him stood Cap Strawn and Holly. Her eyes were glistening, and it came to him after a moment that she'd been crying; yet she was no less nice to look upon.

He was, he discovered, pretty well tied up with bandages.

"You're going to be all right," Strawn announced, as if it had to be. He looked haggard and worried, made miserable by self-reproach. "I was watching for Murdine to come down the street . . . and he never did . . . when I saw something moving in the wagon yard. Overstreet's white shirt, I guess.

Gave him away. I hollered . . . tried to warn you, King."

"You did, Cap. You were in the right place."

"Well . . . ," Strawn said, and momentarily King glimpsed again the savagery he'd seen in the wagon yard's streaky light. "Twenty years ago I wasn't."

The scene in the yard jarred into place, awakening a powerful revulsion, and King forced himself to regard Holly. "I hate it for your sake," he told her. "But tell me . . . why . . . why'd he do it?"

"I think I know." She was instantly beside him, kneeling down, her hand seeking his. "I told you Phil asked me to marry him. . . ."

There was an interruption. Ross Murdine entered the room heavily. He placed an envelope in King's hand, murmuring: "We found this on Overstreet. It's yours."

"You know what it is?"

Murdine nodded. "Now the smoke's cleared, tracks look plain enough. Overstreet shot Ed Pittman in the back just to get you sore enough to sign such a deed. Even with you out of the way, it was still binding. Left him in position to dicker a deal with Southwestern."

"I guess it figures. But still, why'd . . . ?"

"King," Holly said impatiently, "I told him no. You hear me, King? I told him no!"

The Homeseekers

Asa Banner started across Summit Street, held up for a wagon, and, as it passed, he saw the catchwords rippling on the patched canvas cover: **Oklahoma or Bust**. But it was the faces that left a wake in his mind. The faraway look of the settler, and his plain-cheeked wife, hoping, too, and the shy, excited children. Afterward he crossed through ankle-deep dust to stand on the boardwalk outside the government Land Office and resume his vigil.

Some minutes later, he made a restless turn inside the crowded, noisy office. "Takes about three days to reach the line by wagon," a clerk was explaining. "After you file your claim, you got six months to settle your family on it. First person on a homestead has first claim. Look for stone markers. Be Land Offices at Guthrie and Kingfisher."

One by one, Asa scanned the sunburned faces and went out.

He watched while the afternoon wore away, while the wagon and horseback traffic thickened and people streamed in and out of the high-fronted stores and milled like cattle on the walks and raised a pall of dust over the broad street. Hawkers peddled water at ten cents a dipper. Men swapped horses. In the plain multitude tenderfeet drew stares, awkward in buckskin jackets, wide hats, and self-consciously toting heavy revolvers in new leather holsters.

Two boys carried a stout box from the City Hotel. Trailing them came a man of lordly air, a derby hat high on his head. He mounted the box and peeled off a bright, impressive map from a large bundle.

"Folks," he announced, his voice like a bugle as he waved the map, "they call it the beautiful land down there . . . the Promised Land . . . and that's what it is." A pause, a deliberate pause. Hundreds of heads turned, and the voice picked up, resonant, convincing. "Finest farm country you ever laid eyes on. Why, they say the climate's a good deal like California's . . . neither too hot nor too cold. You betcha. There's only one drawback . . . and that's water. It's a mite scarce at times. But these maps I have here . . . drawn accordin' to the dee-tailed in-structions of a trusted old Indian scout . . . will show you exactly where the creeks and the springs are. Where the best claims can be found. . . . All yours for just one dollar."

There was an erupting surge toward the map peddler, a chorus of voices. Wood cracked, and he floundered to the walk, swarmed under.

Asa Banner watched without moving, cold to the land hunger that he saw flushing the expectant faces like a high fever. About him, he heard the hum and wrangle of voices from a dozen states. Thousands of homeseekers were camped around Arkansas City. Yesterday and today, riding in from Caldwell, he had seen them all along the rutted road. By the morning of April 22nd, thousands more, afoot, would swell this small Kansas border town in hopes of finding seats on the southbound trains.

Again, he began a round of the stores and livery stables and wagon yards. He moved deliberately, uncomfortable in the suit binding his shoulders, feeling the heavy six-shooter bumping his hip. The broad sturdiness of his body often

forced him to walk sideways through the shifting mass over-
flowing the walks.

At the City Hotel a man wedged in ahead of him. Asa
tapped him on the shoulder. When the man ignored him, Asa
placed a solid hand on his shoulder, sent him spinning off the
walk, and heard the crowd yell approval. Finally, Asa worked
inside to the clerk's desk. The register lay open. He read it
line for line, turning the pages back for a week, and stepped
away, thinking: *No, I won't be foolish enough to sign my real
name. Yet. . . .*

A man with tired, sizing-up eyes nodded to him and murmured: "There's a little game in the back. Like to sit in?"

Asa took an onward step, then swung around. "I might."

"Follow me."

In a smoky room off the hallway, Asa saw four card
players, all strangers, around a table. One put down his hand
and rose, invitation fawning across his pallid features.

"Never mind," Asa told him. "I'm not sitting in." These
vultures were as those he had noticed on the streets, flocked
in to fleece the homesteaders and tenderfeet. Asa turned
toward the door. It was closed and in front of it stood the first
man.

"You're all alike," he ridiculed. "Nobody will take a
sportin' chance any more."

"Call this a chance?" Asa said. "Get away from the door."

Stiffening, the man slid his right hand inside his vest. Asa
stepped forward; the hand fell away. Asa, in close, seized the
man's shoulder and threw him sprawling over a chair, and
jerked open the door and slammed it shut behind him.
Through it he could hear an unbroken cursing, but no one
opened the door.

Going down the hallway, he saw an ample-bosomed
woman regarding him from her doorway. One languid white

hand rested against the doorjamb, the other on her hip.

"What's all the racket?" she asked in an indifferent voice.

"Seems we don't agree," he said, and would have gone on had she not put out her hand, a gesture that was more inquiring than restraining.

She gave him a half smile. The skin under her dark eyes was no longer young, but neither was she as old as she looked. Her red lips were heavy, although well-formed, and her mass of lustrous black hair looked carefully combed. *Once,* he thought, *she had been pretty.*

"Sounded like a rough house," she said, arching her eyes.

"Not much," he said.

"Well, you'll get nothing for your money down there from that two-bit bunch." She darted her scorn in that direction and laid a discerning look upon him. "At first I didn't take you for a farmer, but your hands give you away."

"I *am* a farmer," he said. "A pretty good one, I think."

Something almost forgotten seemed to spring into her face. "I like a man who says what he is," she said on impulse. "Look, I run this place, such as it is. I know people. I'm seldom wrong about men, good or bad. Do . . . you need a grubstake?"

He shook his head no.

"Would . . . would you like to work for me here? Help me run this?"

"I won't be here long."

"Just another homesteader," she sneered, and the liveliness left her face.

"You're wrong there," he said. A thought was enlarging, causing him to wonder why he hadn't asked before. "But maybe you can tell me something."

"Shoot."

"I'm looking for a quick horse trader, four-flusher, and

jackleg lawyer named Harley Cade. Least he calls himself a lawyer." Feeling was seeping into his voice.

Her eyes showed him absolutely nothing, yet he thought her mouth seemed to tighten a trifle. "What do you want with him?"

"It's a private matter," Asa replied.

"Isn't it always?"

"You know him?"

Her enigmatic eyes changed suddenly. "Enough. He'll be in the new town of Mulhall the day of the opening. He may go on to Guthrie. That will be the real town in the territory."

"Depends on the pickings, huh?"

"I didn't say."

"That all?"

"Isn't that enough?"

He spoke his thanks and stepped to the door that opened into the lobby. There he hesitated, hearing the voices and the shufflings and stirrings; together, he thought, they were like a hammering pulse for the restless thousands.

"Maybe you'll come back," she said softly.

He turned and looked at her. It was a long look, and then he went out.

On the morning of the 21st, Asa Banner was riding south toward the starting line, into a greening, grass-rustling world rolling gently away under a bright quilting of wildflowers. Ahead and behind him, he could see a snake line of crawling wagons; their bowed hoods seemed to drift as ships on the emerald prairie sea of the Cherokee Outlet.

A new feeling took hold of him. Everything lay so open and unspoiled after the old Illinois country that he knew. The air had a sweet scent. Now and then, clouds of quail and prairie chickens rose in sudden *whirrings*. A line of trees sketched a creek's distant course, gave the eye a mark against the vast spaciousness. At times his lulled mind wandered to waving wheat and grazing cattle. It was as though he fought a bewitchment, while knowing that none of this waiting land could be his.

At the high-banked Salt Fork of the Arkansas he crossed on planks laid over the railroad bridge. His gelding's running walk soon left the wagons behind. Some miles beyond he came upon a lone covered wagon pulled off the broad trail.

A raw-boned settler, his rapid hammer stroke awkward, pounded the loose tire rim of the right rear wheel. A young woman stood by watching, and out on the prairie a small boy picked flowers.

Asa was nearly past when the pounding ceased and he heard a high curse of pain. He looked back to see the man gripping his left hand. Without hesitating, Asa reined across. "Maybe you folks need some help?" he said.

The woman, embarrassed, said: "He can fix it. Thank you just the same."

Meanwhile, the man continued to press his hand and pump it up and down. "I don't know," he said.

Asa dismounted to examine the wheel and rim. "Felly and spokes need soaking, is all," he said after a bit. "Wood's shrunk. Believe I can get the rim back on for you." With spaced strokes, he drove the rim into place, and seeing a roll of barbed wire tied to the underside of the wagon, he bent and broke sections of it with which he wrapped the iron tire to the wheel. As he did these things so natural for him, he could not fail to note the team of poor bay horses, the patched harness, and the rickety condition of the wagon. It was a hard-used outfit, also worn by neglect.

"Cuss the luck, anyway," the homesteader said, surveying Asa's finished work. His lean jaws moved, and his stooped shoulders slumped even more. When he spoke he had a way of pushing out his lower lip, giving it a pendulous suggestion of chronic defeat. A moodiness, a discontent, lay behind his dark eyes.

"You'll make it to the line before dark," Asa assured him.

"Just my luck to have another breakdown."

Asa had mounted when the young woman said: "Dell, I believe you forgot to thank him." And to Asa, in apology: "I'm Emily Marcum. This is my brother, Dell Sutton."

"Half-brother, you mean." Sutton scowled.

She might not have heard him as she said cheerfully: "And that's Billy. We're all obliged to you."

"That's not necessary. I'm Asa Banner, folks. Good luck."

He held up still a moment longer, seeing her gray dress, pale from many washings, her heavy shoes, and the reddish color of her hands, and in her tanned face small wrinkles which should not have been there—for, he decided, she wasn't more than twenty-five. Her eyes were between blue and violet, and she wore her auburn hair pulled back and knotted at her neck. The prairie breeze shaped the long dress about her slim body. But his strongest impression was of her calm and unwavering cheerfulness, which he kept remembering as he rode along.

Later, he discovered black dots moving in the far green distance, some in bunches, like milling cattle spread over the prairie, and among them a range of low white hillocks, some swaying, some still. Riding nearer, he caught a remote drone, like that of bees swarming around a hollow tree. Nearer yet, he heard the drone turn into clatters and rumbles, into voices carrying across open country, and the hillocks became wagon tops.

East and west, as far as he could see, the prairie and wooded draws bloomed with snowy wagon tops and tents.

Everyone seemed to observe an invisible line; gazing south, he understood why. Out there blue-clad cavalrymen rode back and forth or had posted themselves, guarding the free country until high noon tomorrow, when they would release the tide of homeseekers.

Leaving the main trail, Asa clattered across a rock branch and, searching once more, rode slowly west through an army of parked wagons, buggies, carts, and horsemen. Retracing his way, he scouted east past the branch for several miles, without luck again, and swung west, thinking to water his horse and make camp. By now the sun was low. Smoke from early supper fires trailed keen, hungering smells across the cool spring air. He sighted low clouds banking in the west. Rain, maybe.

He had not reached the branch when his attention went to a solitary wagon halted on the main trail. The miserable, drooping team looked familiar, and on the wagon's right side three figures, one a child, stood around the rear wheel. Asa pulled up, recalling the man. What was his name? Sutton . . . Dell Sutton? It was much easier to remember the woman's name . . . Emily Marcum. Well, her brother was a grumbler and a leaner. Reflecting on that thought, Asa passed west to the rocky branch and watered his horse.

He was eating his supper of hot coffee, bacon, and cold biscuits when Dell Sutton drove his limping wagon some rods down the wooded branch and unhitched. Minutes later Asa saw Sutton chopping on a large elm, using a hand axe. Soon Sutton's sister appeared. She shook her head at his clumsy efforts and pointed to a sapling. When Asa looked again, Sutton was struggling to lash the cut sapling under the right rear axle.

Asa experienced a vague hesitation. If you gave a leaner a hand, he just leaned that much harder on you. Now he saw

Emily Marcum leave her cooking to help her brother. Soon after, Sutton stood back to watch her.

In disgust Asa set down his tin coffee cup and walked across. It was almost as though Dell Sutton had expected him, for he said: "I remember you said soak the wheel. That's what I aim to do, if I ever get the blamed thing off."

"Let me see what I can find," Asa said, and went back up the draw. He returned carrying flat rocks that he piled under the axle. Two more trips and the axle rested on a stout base. Asa removed the nut from the hub, pulled the wheel free, hammered the rim on, and rolled the wheel to the little stream for soaking.

Not until he was returning to the wagon did his sense of irritation catch up with him. While he had labored, Dell Sutton had observed and commented on the sorry state of his luck.

"We're obliged to you again, Mister Banner," Emily Marcum said. "Won't you stay for supper?"

"Thanks," Asa said. "I've had mine."

"Will you come for breakfast?"

There was, Asa thought, little or no resemblance between her and Sutton; somehow he was glad to discover that difference, and he wanted no more of Sutton's company. Other perceptions caused him to delay. These people were bone poor. Asa had felt it in the lightness of the wagon when removing the wheel, and he saw it in the meager supper being prepared, and in the woman's drawn face, in the boy's, and he was angered because he could not change it.

And so he declined and turned on his heel before she could insist.

Asa Banner watched evening let down, spreading rich purple over the scented prairie, and he heard the voices of the camped multitude, clear and full of hope:

We'll cross the mighty river
We'll cross the river Jordan

It occurred to him that those were family groups singing; strangers only hours ago, now drawn together by the promise of new land and beginning life over again. For some there wouldn't be enough homesteads to go around. Yet tonight, he thought, everyone was rich, lifted up, and made young again by the seeking. Now and then, from another direction, he caught strains of banjo music and barroom verses about a girl waiting at the end of the Chisholm Trail. He smiled to himself. Cowboys. They rode fast horses; they knew where the best claims lay. He could feel the wish to be one of them.

Unable to resist the voices, he strolled over to a large fire that the singers ringed. Standing back in the shadows, he saw toil traced in the upturned faces—chinch bugs and drought, good times and lean times. Among the faces were those of Emily Marcum and Billy. Around Asa men smoked and talked of tomorrow. He heard a familiar, discouraging voice: "Look at them clouds a-buildin' up. We're in for a bad storm, I tell you. Listen to that thunder." It was Dell Sutton.

At that moment the voices soared louder. Conversation trailed off. A light breeze sprang up, damp, rain-laden, its touch uneasy on the face. A common feeling seemed to seize the singers. A strange excitement.

Asa Banner felt it likewise. He had the unreality of seeing actors on a stage, of being affected despite his detachment.

Movement rippled through the little crowd. A high-shouldered man making his way toward the fire. A rake-handle shape, he was, greasy black hair dangling to this shoulders, his eyes wild and darting in the uncertain light. He mouthed something and waved his long arms, prophetic, ominous.

116

Asa made out—"Hellfire and doom!" That was all. Suddenly the stranger took long-striding steps back the way he had materialized. The crowd shrank away, opening a path. In moments he disappeared.

Just then the first spattering raindrops fell. A woman near Asa screamed and touched hands to her face. He saw her jerk her hands down and stare at them. He saw her swift fear, as of seeing blood, and her melting relief, as if a spell had passed.

Pealing thunder scattered these weather-wise people. Before they could reach their wagons and teams, gusts of wind lashed the camp. Whipping canvas tops slapped and ripped.

Asa started forward. A running man slammed into him, rushed on. Asa hurried across. When he found Emily Marcum, she was standing still, shielding Billy's face with her hands. Wordlessly Asa took her arm. She turned at his touch, and in the light from the flashing sky he could tell that she expected Dell Sutton.

By the time they neared the wagon, the wind was hurling rain shot against their wet faces. Out of the flickering darkness, Dell Sutton staggered, hands protecting his face. Asa left them and bent on toward his picketed horse.

He had covered but few rods when a crash and cries shot up behind him. He stopped. Another cry, a woman's, wheeled him about. He ran back to find the wagon blown over and the woman and boy struggling to lift it off Sutton, who was shouting at them.

Asa knelt, worked his hands under the sideboard. Heaving and grunting, he strained upward, and Sutton scrambled out and stood up gripping his right arm. Asa forgot him while he set about righting the light wagon.

And then, as suddenly as it had struck, the prairie storm rumbled off, gone. The moon slid out, big and clear.

Afterward, in the lantern light, it was Emily who pushed

the flat rocks in place every time Asa lifted the axle up another notch.

"You did a right good job," Dell Sutton said, sounding contrite.

Asa, soaked through, walked past without speaking. Finding dry clothing in his bedroll, he spread out his poncho, rolled in his blanket, and slept.

A bright morning dawned. After last night's violence, Asa reckoned superstitious settlers would see the wide blue sky and the sparkling prairie as good omens. Yet by noon the frontier would vanish, and a kind of regret had its way with him.

While he gathered firewood, figures moved into his vision from down the draw: Emily Marcum and young Billy. She lifted her long skirts above the wet grass. Pleasure smoothed her face as she looked off across the open country. Her heavy shoes bothered him. *No woman,* he thought, *should have to wear such footgear.*

"We want you to have breakfast with us," she greeted him. At his hesitation she said earnestly: "We've put you to a heap of trouble, Mister Banner."

"Not at all," he said, and changed his mind then. "I'll be glad to come. Thank you. And the name is Asa."

At breakfast Dell Sutton, his arm in a sling, appeared to enjoy indisposition. He talked freely of the day's prospects. "Emily will have to handle the team," he said. "I can't do a thing. She's some woman, Mister Banner. First thing she did this mornin' was put that wheel on all by herself. . . . Reckon you've got a certain part of the country in mind for your claim?"

"I'm not here for land," Asa said.

"Well, I sure am. All I been thinkin' about for a year. A

body gets tired of keepin' store. No future. Land's the thing."

"It can be a hard taskmaster, too," Asa said reminiscently. "Breaking this prairie sod won't be easy."

"Now Emily's man was a right good hand at that. She lost him last year . . . pneumonia. That's another reason why we're here. I want her and the boy to have something."

Breakfast over, Dell Sutton drifted off to visit his neighbors. Asa could hear his nasal voice lifted high, recounting the story of his storm-toppled wagon and his miraculous escape from serious injury. It was unlikely that Sutton had been an important man in the past or would be in the future. But today, sharing in the seeking and hoping, he was no less than the other far-eyed comers.

As he thanked Emily Marcum for the meal, Asa saw a question in her eyes.

"It's time to say good bye again," she said, smiling a little. "I hope we can homestead near a town, so there will be a school for Billy."

"Mulhall will be the nearest town from here," he told her. "That's southeast. The railroad goes through it. Take bottom land if you can, for wood, water, and pasture."

"Mulhall? So you're going there?"

"Yes."

"Then?"

"I'll go home."

Her thoughtful expression formed. But she said no more, and he walked back to his camp, aware of a vague discontent.

While the morning advanced, Asa Banner could sense the jostling impatience of the homeseekers. He packed up and rode to the line. Every tent was down. Hitched teams stood waiting. Men huddled in little groups, gesturing, pointing south, southeast, southwest, scanning maps. When a stranger approached, the talk switched abruptly. Almost every man carried a weapon. From saddles hung sharpened stakes with flags; these would be driven into the ground as the first act toward claiming a tract.

As the sun rose toward high noon, Asa saw Emily Marcum drive the wagon in close to the line. Billy sat between her and Sutton, who was reared back, head high. Asa looked at his watch: eleven twenty. Now the crowd flowed forward to pack the starting place. Men and women on horses, in wagons, fringed surreys, on foot, a few on high-wheeled bicycles, some pushed carts.

A flurry of action ruffled the open prairie. Two cavalrymen were escorting a protesting rider back to the line. He shook his fist at them as they rode away, and shouting settlers in turn cursed him. He displayed his disdain by halting rods in front of the others, whereupon determined homesteaders, all armed, marched out and forced him to ride behind the line.

Asa heard a man complain: "Another damned Sooner. They been sneakin' in for weeks. By God, it ain't fair. Us folks who made the government open up this country ought to get choice quarter sections without a run."

Just minutes now. A lull settled. Men on high-strung horses lined up near the front, jockeyed for position. Asa heard a throat-torn shout, a warning shout. Immediately the troopers fired pistols, and with a rising roar the tide of settlers spilled over the green prairie. All at once the voices dulled, muffled in the massive rumbling and bumping. A river of yellow fog enveloped swaying wagons and buggies, turned fleeing horsemen into quirting specters.

Asa lost sight of the Sutton wagon. His own horse was galloping, for he had let it go when the line surged. Already some homesteaders were jumping down to plant their fluttering flags. A train hooted cheerfully. Far away Asa saw its scribbling smoke. He pulled in his horse and angled that way.

About that time he picked up the Sutton wagon again, noticeable because it held a slanting course to his left while other homeseekers were hurrying south and southwest. Emily Marcum had the poor team trotting steadily. He was suddenly troubled. A pity if in taking his advice she found no free land.

He followed the wagon, staying well back. He kept telling himself there was no hurry for him, that he was unmoved by what he saw. Still, when he turned his head and his eyes met the glittering face of the prairie beckoning in all directions, he understood precisely why the movers and campers and down-and-outers had come. A little later he stopped to take the six-shooter from his bedroll and belt it around him. It still felt unnatural and cumbersome, so strange to him and his way of living that he had not worn it since Arkansas City.

Now the sun was slipping into afternoon. Ahead the prairie, rising, dipping, swayed again to straggling creek timber, and there, like a tired white bird, rested one lone wagon, small against the sweeping green of the rich bottom land. The Sutton wagon. Beside it stood flag and stake.

A quick pleasure coursed through Asa Banner, and he rode faster toward the wagon, the uncropped grass brushing his horse's belly. Dell Sutton waved in recognition and ran out to meet him.

"Mister Banner!" he shouted. "We've got us a claim!" Sutton's arm swung free of its sling. His voice had a new ring. He stood straighter. His black eyes flashed. Triumph flushed his lean face. He looked ten years younger.

"Fine," Asa said, sharing Sutton's elation. "Fine."

"We've checked the markers," Emily Marcum said. "It's ours." Her eyes were shining. Young Billy was jumping up and down and exclaiming.

"See that big burr oak down there?" Sutton asked, pointing to the creek. "I'll dig my dug-out there. Gonna start right away."

As Asa turned to see, two men trailed out of the brush and timber masking the small creek. Both carried rifles. They tramped to the wagon.

"Looks like you folks are a little late," the lead man said. He shoved his head forward, his heavy jaw set. A bib-like beard covered the upper buttons of his shirt. Not a cruel-faced individual, but his eyes were shrewd and he backed up his belligerent manner by planting his boots wide and showing off the menace of his thick, sloping shoulders.

Dell Sutton's face was ash white. "There's my stake," he pointed. "Where's yours?"

The bearded man inclined his head vaguely to the east.

"It wasn't there when I walked over the claim," Sutton said. "And I didn't see you."

"That's not my look-out. This man will vouch for me. Now get off."

Asa waited for Dell Sutton to back down, and he saw Sutton's head sag bit by bit and he watched him stare at the ground. Sutton's mouth was trembling. His sister watched with an expression akin to sorrow and resignation.

Inch by inch, Sutton brought his head up. His lips were still quivering when he spoke: "No . . . this land is mine. I won't get off." His hands clenched. Sweat beaded his ridged forehead. He stepped forward.

"By God . . . ," the other man blurted, astonished. He made a sudden motion with the rifle. Emily screamed.

Asa jabbed heels to the gelding, at the same instant seeing the man's startled eyes above the mossy beard, just before he heard and felt the jar of his horse's forequarters knock the man down and loose from his rifle.

The second man ran dodging. Asa buck-jumped the gelding alongside and leaned low, tore the rifle free, hurled it into the tall grass, and reined around. That was when, late, he remembered his pistol, still holstered, and he touched it. He looked up to find Emily Marcum's eyes on him.

Sutton had the first intruder's rifle and was guarding him.

"I'll file a contest," the man swore.

"You'll play hell," Asa said. "You're Sooners . . . you sneaked in early and hid out. I'm a witness for these folks. Now hit the grit."

The two drifted away in the direction of Mulhall. Dell Sutton took his eyes off them and thoughtfully considered the rifle, as if surprised at himself, and leaned it against a wagon wheel.

"You didn't bluff," Asa said, "so they won't bother you again." He eyed the sun and headed his horse southeast.

"Do you have to go?" Emily Marcum asked.

"I've come a long way."

She came even with his stirrup, and he saw her open expression. "Why do you think you have to kill someone? You're no gunman."

He had an answer, and yet somehow he did not, and so he made no reply.

Mulhall was an anthill writhing under the hot springtime sun. Frantic hammerings rose above the din. Flimsy, frame buildings stood finished, clean and yellow; others were skeletons, taking form even as he watched, and the smell of the newly cut lumber flavored the red dust. Tents fronted on the wide street and grew on it as well, seemingly planted without reason, and their white tops speckled the distance on all sides of the brash settlement.

Asa Banner passed through the restless throng to the end

of the street and rode back. Next to the Boomer Saloon, on a vacant lot, two men in derby hats occupied chairs behind boxes on which hung lettered signs: **Law Office**.

Asa's lips flattened. He rode faster. One man he dismissed at once. It was the other one, back turned, talking, gesturing, who looked faintly familiar. The man turned around. He wore a full beard, and he was heavy. Asa reined up, his tension ebbing. How did you find one man among thousands?

Not long afterward he rode to the depot, tied up, and mounted the crowded platform. "When's the next train?" he asked.

"Ten minutes."

Inside the box-like building disgruntled homeseekers pushed and shouted for tickets to Guthrie and Oklahoma City. Watching the jostling line, as he had the faces on the platform, he sensed the futility of his coming here.

A roly-poly, bush-bearded man turned, head bent over money and ticket. He carried a carpetbag. The gray eyes under the derby hat found Asa briefly, flecked away, before the man stepped past.

Something tugged on Asa's mind, a troubling elusiveness. He jerked. That fellow! He was one of the lawyers set up in business only minutes ago by the saloon.

Asa was rushing out, drawn by a thing he couldn't connect. The packed crowd around the door blocked his way, hid his view. Boots rapped the platform on his right. Elbowing a path, Asa gained the end of the building, but the face wasn't there. He jumped to the ground and ran to the rear of the depot. Just beyond, a stout figure was lumbering across the open prairie.

In pounding strides Asa closed in. The man whirled and stopped, feigning surprise, a near-handsome man with a fleshy face. A knife sheath rode on his belt.

Asa still wasn't convinced. He flicked out his left hand, knocked the derby off, and then he knew, and he saw that knowledge strike across Harley Cade's eyes.

Asa drew his pistol. "You almost fooled me," he hacked. "That beard . . . that hat . . . and fat as a hog." He eared back the hammer.

Cade's skin showed chalk above the thick brown beard. His voice sounded hollow: "Remember . . . your sister . . . she came with me."

"She did. But you left her to die in Caldwell. She wrote me. She and the baby were both dying when I got there . . . right after you pulled out."

"I'm here to make a stake. I was goin' back."

"You're lying. You saw me on the street back there. You're running."

Cade's eyes bugged. "What you aim to do?"

"Make you pay up, now. Great big."

Asa Banner raised the pistol. His face knotted. For long moments he held the pistol on Harley Cade, not understanding why he couldn't kill a man who deserved killing. Of a sudden he holstered the handgun, confused by the struggle taking place inside himself, unable to figure himself.

Next thing he knew, Cade was digging inside his coat. Asa crashed into him, and he heard Cade grunt and the *thud* of Cade's revolver on the grass. Asa smashed Cade's face, a savage blow that squirted blood. Cade, his face contorted, his eyes wild, lunged back with drawn knife, and Asa saw in him the wish to kill.

That was when Asa Banner drew his pistol, tortuously slow at best, and shot Harley Cade. The slug drove Cade backward one step; his mouth opened in total astonishment before he fell.

Around Asa, quickly, excited voices spoke, and he was

conscious of faces as in a blur, none distinct. A man said: "We saw him come at you with that knife. You had to do it. What was it over . . . a claim?"

Asa was too numb and sick to speak. Where was the righteous satisfaction he was supposed to feel? He had none whatever. Presently a train whistled, and he stood alone by the depot platform. A consciousness grew. By nightfall the shooting would be all but forgotten, one of the many violent episodes that the mighty stream of the day's events had swept under.

Another thought flared as light streaking across the darkness of his mind. It warmed him. He mounted and saddled northwest.

Emily Marcum looked up from her cooking when he was yet some distance from the wagon, an alertness that told him she had been watching. She came running through the tall virgin grass, pulling at her skirts, now pushing at a strand of hair falling across her forehead. She ran until he reined in before her. Her eyes, sweeping over him, held an enormous relief.

"You better know this," he said, and hesitated. "I found out I didn't want to kill a man, after all. Then I had to."

She stood quite straight and still, the soft swell of her breasts rising and falling, a tall young woman whose sudden exertion had flushed hidden prettiness to her plain face, whose parted mouth framed a sweet-lipped gravity.

"I believe you," she said, and, as he swung down from the saddle and he saw the giving and the pain for him, he felt a powerful shock, and he knew there never would be an end for either of them.

Mystery of the Mountain Light

Larry Morgan drove the pickup past the dark ranch house, parked under the shed, and, coming out, stood in the moon-drenched yard, watching the teasing flicker of lightning off southwest. Heat lightning, his grandfather Morgan had called it, and that didn't mean needed rain.

He turned toward the house, yawning after the drive into town to see the late movie. From habit he glanced at the black mass of the Wichita Mountains towering east of the house, walking on as he did, only to face abruptly around, a strange sensation kneading his backbone. For a count or so he lost sight of it, but it came on again, back in the mountains, a single beam of light probing powerfully, high up, among the timber and rocks. Larry hesitated no longer, running to the porch, jerking open the back screen door, and calling his grandfather.

"What is it?" Junius Morgan, who rose every morning at five o'clock, sounded wide awake.

"The lights you told me about . . . I can see 'em up in the mountains!"

"Them again," said Junius, quickly pulling on trousers and stomping into his boots. He paused just long enough to snatch his .30-30 saddle gun off the wall before he rushed out into the yard.

Hurrying behind him, Larry saw the relentless, yellow eye

of the light still searching. For a vivid moment he imagined a wild animal caught in the blinding glare, motionless and helpless, an easy target. Now the eye steadied, became fixed, and he gave a start as he heard a distant shot reverberate through the hills.

"By Jacks, I got a mind to ride up there!" his grandfather said bitterly.

"Let the game warden handle it," Larry urged, sensing the threat of violence, for Junius Morgan had lived the hard, free life of a roving cowboy in his younger days. "Can't we talk to him?"

"Talk to *him* again! I'm talked out!" And suddenly the old man, in frustration, began firing the rifle into the air, as fast as he could work the lever and pull the trigger. The rank smell of gunpowder stung Larry's nostrils, and his ears rang. As the hammer snapped on empty, the light went out.

Soon after daylight they saddled horses and rode toward the nearby mountains where Junius pastured his whitefaces, an almost daily ride since Larry had arrived in June to spend the summer. On the slope overlooking the flat where the Morgan Ranch lay he could see the hard-scrabble Kelsey Ranch, a knot of paintless buildings and sheds, makeshift fences and corrals. As they entered the mountains, rocky crags rose steeply on both sides, clad in blackjacks, oaks, and elms; maples and a few cottonwoods stood in the draws. It was not at all the prairie landscape most people visualized at the mention of Oklahoma.

Usually Junius talked as he rode along, pointing out the various grasses and landmarks, a peak or an old rock corral or the remains of a homesteader's dug-out. You found grama grass on the high places, he said. Big and little bluestem reached their peaks during the spring and summer months. Larry's favorite was the low-growing, curly variety named after the buffalo.

So by now he knew that the Wichita Mountains possessed riches not evident to the untrained eye; here where the tall prairie grasses and those of the short grass country mingled in luxuriant confusion, when one grass thinned out, another was always coming on. Furthermore, Junius said, grassy benches, unseen from the valley floor up which they now rode, flanked the sides of the mountains. High up there the big elk lay in thick timber during the hot summer days.

Of the ten or fifteen Junius was protecting on the ranch, one was a large and very proud bull nicknamed Big Boy. Earlier in the summer Larry had glimpsed him clattering down a slope in long, powerful strides, unmindful of the rocks and brush, his straw-colored rump patch bobbing, his magnificent head thrown back, his great antlers like trees growing out of his head, every point like polished ivory. In September, when the mating season began, Big Boy's bugling challenges would make the valley ring.

That was the day Junius had explained about the poachers, how they slipped into the mountains and spotlighted game, quartered and packed out the kill on horses, sold it by the pound or the carcass. There was also a market for racks or antlers. Big Boy's handsome head would bring additional money. Meanwhile, Junius said, complaints to the state hadn't stopped the poaching or even slowed it.

Larry knew from reading that poaching is one of the oldest forms of crime. The great Khans of Asia had laws punishing the stealing of game by death. Legend said that Shakespeare, as a boy, had poached rabbits from the land of English lords. Even now, it seemed, with supermarkets at every crossroads, poaching paid enough to tempt criminals.

Junius said little this morning. He looked grim as he rode, the carbine in a long boot under his right leg. Although not a

129

large man, he conveyed the impression of size and strength despite his age, because he still had a horseman's lean hips and waist. A graying man who wasn't supposed to ride snuffy young horses any more, but did; who had been told by the doctor not to attempt the work of two men, but did. Larry thought he saw a new intensity in his grandfather's eyes. A light blue they were, close to a slate gray, in them the directness of a man who had met violence in his own time and not backed away. A man of the story-book West.

They rode through little bunches of fat whiteface cows and their frisky spring calves, and reached a meadow-like stretch where the breeze off the grasses rolled sweet and cool. Ahead, up a rocky slope, buzzards wheeled and dived.

Junius Morgan spurred faster, taking the slope in a horse-grunting rush and coming upon a narrow bench deep in grass, and there he got down, his face taut.

"They got an elk, all right," he announced as Larry caught up. "A cow to boot."

Larry looked, turned still with shock and angry revulsion, yet aware of relief, in a way, because it wasn't Big Boy as he had feared.

"Just took the hindquarters," Junius said in a voice dry as prairie dust. "Looks like somebody got in a hurry." He bent suddenly and picked up a butcher knife crusted with blood. His square, brown face took on a deeper resolve, and he rode down the slope and commenced to circle, looking for tracks. He reined up after a short distance. Grimness ran quickly across his face, and he rode on, bent over to study the ground.

Now Larry saw the prints of hoofs. But it was the high, thick grass that made the trail unmistakable, still bent and streaked after the passage of horses and men last night.

They followed the tracks to a barbed-wire fence marking the limit of Morgan land. Here, Larry could read the signs as well as Junius: someone had pulled the metal staples from the posts, stood on the strands of wire while the pack animals stepped across, and left the fence sagging.

They crossed as the poachers had and pursued the tracks through a gap in the mountains to a dirt road. There horse tracks made a pocked clutter among tire marks, vanished, and then the tires went down the road toward the main highway a mile away.

"Pickup and horse trailer," Junius decided. "Let's go fix that fence."

They were past the bench where the elk lay, and Larry could see far away the top of the Morgan ranch house as a tiny white chip afloat on the green sea of the flat, when he sighted two riders approaching. One rode a lazy gray mule, the other a gaunt bay horse that looked half starved.

Junius jumped his mount forward. Both riders pulled up.

"You're trespassing," Junius told them, blocking the cow trail.

"Don't you know your neighbor?" asked the horseman. He was a lank-jawed man, round-shouldered and dirtier than necessary. Everything about him spoke of hard use, from his slouch hat to his run-down boots, poor saddle, and his miserable horse.

"I know you, Kelsey," Junius replied. "And I know Wardlow there when I see him. What're you men doing here?"

"Fool milk cow didn't come up . . . figured she'd be on your pasture," Kelsey said.

"I keep all my fences tight. Nothing gets in or out, 'less somebody lets down the wire . . . like back there."

"You ain't seen my cow?"

"Just a cow elk . . . shot last night and butchered!" Junius reached into his saddlebag and held up the crusted knife, shaking it at Kelsey. "This what you came back for?"

A look of injured innocence filled Kelsey's face, growing until Larry felt an impulsive sympathy for him. "You accusin' *me?*" Kelsey protested.

"If the shoe fits . . . wear it. Now get off my land. Both of you!"

Kelsey showed more hurt than anger. "Was hopin' you'd be neighborly," he complained, and reined back the way he had come.

But Wardlow held up, and Larry looked at the mild-appearing man of slight build and placid blue eyes, dressed in worn khaki shirt and trousers, chimney-pot hat and heavy work shoes. According to Junius, Wardlow was regarded as a peculiar individual and had shown up last spring. He "worked around," hunted some, and never bothered anyone. And lately he'd bought the mule, which to any cowman was a ridiculous riding animal.

"Didn't mean to trespass," Wardlow said in apology. "Wanted to see you anyway, Mister Morgan. Wondered if you could use a hand? I'm a hard worker."

"Don't need anybody," Junius snapped.

"Sure much obliged to you just the same," Wardlow said politely. "Sure am." Touching heels to the mule's flanks, he went bumping after Kelsey.

The two were scarcely beyond earshot when Larry spoke. "Granddad, you don't know Kelsey did it. Yet you accused him?"

"Didn't deny it, did he?"

"But he's such a poor-looking man," Larry said sympathetically.

Junius turned slowly. "Where your eyes, boy? Guess you didn't notice that TV aerial and nice pickup as we rode past his house? He's even got a phone."

"What about Wardlow?"

"About the same litter, I figure. Camps on the creek near Kelsey's place."

It was past noon before they returned to the ranch. Junius got on the phone immediately to the office of Smiley Bone, the district game warden. Around three o'clock a dusty sedan drove up, and a round-bodied man got out rather clumsily.

"Now just what's all the trouble, Junius?" he boomed, showing a smile that said everything would be all right. As he walked toward the house, the flabbiness of the man seemed to drop away, and Larry noticed the thick chest and shoulders and neck, and the rough, heavy hands.

"Same as before . . . poachers." Junius began telling him what had happened, omitting no details.

Bone sat down on the edge of the porch, took out a notebook and pencil stub, and now and then wrote a little, nodding all the while, his pink, smooth face settled in an expression of enduring patience.

"I know, I know," he said, when Junius had finished. "One man tries to build on nature, another tears it smack down. Human nature. Trouble is, you got to have evidence before you haul off and file charges. That's serious business."

"I understand all about that," Junius assured him.

Bone's face let in the first dent of disagreement, yet a tolerant one. "You forgot what I did last summer, when I lay out there three nights straight, an' nobody showed up?"

"I remember. I appreciate it."

"Then what do you 'spect me to do, Junius?"

"Get off your stump, Smiley. Why, it's common talk in town you can buy an elk for a hundred dollars. More, if the order's for a big bull elk with a nice rack."

Bone elevated his gaze, his eyes acquiring an infinite forbearance. "Easier said than done, Junius. Any suspects?"

Junius hesitated. "Guess I'd better not accuse anybody 'less I'm mighty sure of what I'm sayin'."

"That's right," Bone agreed, rising. "Well, I'll check around some more." He idled out to the car, opened the door, and held a look on Junius. "You know, it's plumb dangerous staggerin' around in those mountains after dark. Man could get shot for an elk, couldn't he, in that kinda country?"

He waved as he drove off, and, Larry saw, he was grinning broadly again, an unpleasant grin.

As Bone turned into the section-line road, a rider was jogging along it. Larry saw Bone stop, chat a bit, and drive on.

A little later Wardlow rode up to the house on his drowsy mule. "Good afternoon," he nodded around. Junius barely bent his head. "Just wondered," Wardlow inquired politely, "if I might borrow a dab of coffee and flour? Sure would appreciate it."

Without hesitation, Junius turned to Larry. "Get him some." When Larry returned with two paper sacks, Wardlow thanked him again and again and Junius the same. Junius, Larry observed, hadn't yet invited Wardlow to dismount.

"Sure much obliged to you, Mister Morgan," Wardlow kept on. "I'll pay this back just as soon as I can hustle into town. Sure do appreciate it. Meantime, if you need any help around your place, let me know."

Junius gave no response. Wardlow was bobbing down the road when Junius let go his cattleman's exasperation: "Any man who rides a mule is sicky nice and borrows!"

Twice a week Larry and Junius rode the fence line that enclosed the rugged mountain pasture.

Larry suspected that his grandfather checked the stout barrier more than needed, that he took the long rides chiefly for the pleasure of looking at the cattle, of which he never tired, and observing nature in general, enjoying the same places over and over as he would the company of old friends.

Not many days after the game warden's call, they were riding fence again. Something reddish brown against the green of the pasture attracted Larry. He turned and pointed. Junius was already looking; together they hastened over.

It was a pretty whiteface heifer, stiff in the grass.

Junius took a quick look, swung down, and just stood there, hands on hips, a terrible expression stamping his face. "Didn't see a light last night," he said, puzzled. "Didn't hear a shot."

"We were late getting back," Larry said. "Car trouble. Remember?"

In his deepening fury, Junius Morgan reacted on instinct. He got on his horse and started to move.

Larry's attention was still on the heifer. "Look!" he called, as the meaning burst through him that both had missed. "They didn't take the meat."

Junius reined about and stared, his lips compressing. "So they didn't," he said in the quietest of voices. "How do you figure it? A stray shot?"

"It's a warning," Larry said soberly. "That's what it is. The poachers' way of telling us to let 'em alone or. . . ."

"Somebody will get hurt," Junius finished. "Well, we're gonna see about that and before long, too."

For some evenings he took the saddle gun, rode out, and posted himself in the timber, refusing to let Larry accompany him and not returning until well past midnight. The strain began to tell on him. "Guess I'm too old to bust brush any more," he said. "I'll stick in a while."

To Larry's immense relief nothing happened. He dreaded leaving his grandfather alone, and so he put off going home and stayed later than he ever had.

A somber lull seemed to settle over the mountains. No lights searched the high places. Late August showers greened the pasture and turned the mornings sparkling. Riding out early, Larry felt the first faint chill of early fall. He experienced a pang as he sensed the end of his last summer on the ranch and a growing up within himself. Before long he'd be leaving to start his senior year in high school.

One morning he heard a stirring blast from far up in the mountains. A clear, vibrant note, rising higher and higher, challenging the entire valley, and ending in a shrill bugling.

Junius, his eyes bright with excitement, jumped up from the breakfast table, and Larry followed him outside.

"That's old Big Boy himself," Junius explained. "I know his call. A young elk makes a whistling sound. He's early this year, though. Maybe it's the cool weather."

Thereafter, Junius became extremely busy. He took the .30-30 wherever he went, and at dark every night he drove away, across the flat, he said, to sit up with an old friend who was seriously ill and needed help.

Two days before Larry was to leave he sat alone on the long porch, watching the stars glitter over the dark mountains. The late night was still, broken only by the chorus of crickets and the occasional passing of a car on the section-line road. A lone light shone in the distance, a feeble glow at the Kelsey Ranch on the slope.

Drowsiness stole over Larry. He yawned and stood up to go to bed, yet reluctant, and in that moment he saw a long, yellow ray of light pierce the darkness of the mountain valley. He turned rock still, feeling a mixture of protest and fear forming in his stomach and rising in his throat. For Junius would be home any minute, and Larry knew that his grandfather, in his desperate mood, would rush up there if he saw the light.

He hurried inside, found his single shot .22 and a box of longs, dashed out and, throwing a hasty look at the dark road, began striding for the mountains that loomed ahead.

His grandfather said the Wichitas had many voices. Climbing the rough cattle trail in the clear night, Larry could understand now as the faint breeze rustled the dry oak leaves into a whimpering dance, and whippoorwills uttered plaintive calls on both sides of him, and nighthawks made swift, brushing sounds.

He seemed to follow the trail for an endless time, alternately concerned that the poachers had escaped and apprehensive that he might suddenly encounter them. He paused, his shirt soaked from his rapid walk. He heard nothing new, only the bird sounds. He covered another fifty yards, and, as he strained his senses, he picked up a muffled clatter ahead, the dull stumbling of a horse traveling over rocks, an unshod horse, and people who rode the mountains didn't shoe their horses.

Larry stepped faster, until caution pressed him still again, and, looking up, he saw a circle of light seeking out the mountainside on his left. He closed in, not slowing until he made out the high, dark shapes of horses, and one man working the searchlight and another, the hunter, watching close by. A third figure held the horses.

It hadn't occurred to Larry exactly what he would do, other than try to stop the poachers or capture them, somehow. Now that he stood so near them he froze in his tracks. He felt paralyzed as the ring of light searched lower down the mountain and swept deliberately across a grassy, open place, wavered and swung back, and settled like a noose over a great tawny creature with forested antlers.

Larry's mouth opened in unconscious protest. He broke forward, running. He heard a shout tear from his throat, and somewhere to his right, in the timber, the frantic pounding of boots. Before him, suddenly, he saw everything, savage and unreal. The rifleman was whirling toward him, and, as instinct drove him to the rocky ground, Larry caught sight of Smiley Bone's desperate face in the powerful glare of the searchlight.

And to Larry's astonishment the man holding the horses was running toward Bone, shouting: "Drop it . . . you're both under arrest!" Bone's rifle clattered down. But the man by the searchlight lunged across, and there was a rolling scuffle on the ground.

Bone was groping for his rifle when a figure ran clumping from the trees, his cool voice ordering everyone to stand still, and Larry saw his grandfather advance into the light with the saddle gun.

A long shape got up first and stood slouched, the bold light exposing his pinched features. It was Kelsey. Larry, going forward, stared at the second man. It was Wardlow. He held a revolver in a steady hand.

"You . . . you stand back there, too," Junius puffed at Wardlow.

Wardlow had shed his polite meekness. His voice sounded crisp: "I'm not with them. I'm an agent from the State Wildlife Commission."

"You?"

"You can see my credentials." Wardlow tapped his shirt pocket. "And you saw me place 'em under arrest. You and the young man will be witnesses."

Bone was edging in. "I can explain everything," he said, and stooped suddenly for his rifle again. But Wardlow's warning stopped him, and that ended the whole thing.

Junius stood slumped in fatigue. Only then did he take notice of Larry. "I finally got smart," he said. "Kelsey can see our house from his, so he knew whenever we drove off at night. All he had to do was phone Smiley. . . . That's why I kept going after dark. I'd drive down the road apiece, turn off my lights, come back past the house, park, and leg it up here to wait. I just about jumped outta my boots when you shouted and I saw who it was in the moonlight. By Jacks, Smiley might 'a' shot you, boy!"

"And all the time I was scared you'd rush up here if I didn't," Larry said.

The moonlight looked almost like day when they started down the valley with the silent prisoners. Some distance on Larry heard a faint rattle of rocks high overhead on the mountainside. Whatever it was, he and Junius seemed to have the same thought, for his grandfather said, "It's good to know that old Big Boy is still up there."

It was, Larry thought. He'd never felt better in his life.

A Day in the Forest

There in the pooled shadows of the tall forest, alone, naked to his lean waist, he heard only the steady chocking of his axe or the cracking of branches and the thumping crash of a tree when it went down. And blending with those sounds, the sudden whirs and cries of startled birds.

He liked the feel of the axe. It gave him a sense of strength and doing and being. Now he swung with his long arms, swaying his raw-boned body at the hips to add weight to the blow. The blade flashed and bit into the light-brown hide of an oak. Then, jerking upward on the hickory handle, he freed the axe and paused, his mind fixing again on the haunting dream.

A dream, yet not like a dream, so real it was, creeping into his head last night while he lay on his corn-shuck mattress in the cabin's loft and the first timid raindrops tiptoed across the clapboard roof. For just a count or so, no more, he could see as though someone had lit a lamp in his mind—people everywhere he looked, their upturned faces strangely beautiful as they seemed to wait, people beckoning and calling to him, some weeping and then, as though a shutter closed, the vivid scene vanished. Try as he might he couldn't bring it back for a closer size-up, and his hand brushing his eyes came away wet. He was struggling for breath. He had sat up, both fascinated and puzzled, searching the dream for meaning.

Good luck or bad? Good luck or bad? Bitter or sweet? Or did it mean anything?

Now of a sudden he realized that he had been standing in thought for long moments, his great hands still gripping the curved axe handle. He stirred himself and eyed the blade to see if it needed sharpening, which it did not yet, and it occurred to him that when he wasn't plowing or pulling fodder, he was chopping away undergrowth or felling timber to make a clearing or splitting rails for fences. He remembered his first hatchet even before his father, left poor by faulty land titles, had moved the family out of Kentucky, across the Ohio River, into this Indiana wilderness where grapevines as thick as snakes ran from tree to tree and cool shadows never left the forest in summer. "Never cuss a good axe." That was a saying his neighbors had, and a rule they kept, even if your axe slipped and nearly took off your thumb, as had happened once to him.

A powerful hunger seized him. He swept a gauging look up through the broad tangle of branches some sixty feet high, seeing the open face of the Indian-summer sky and pillowed white clouds drifting and the warm eye of the sun. It was a notch past noon. So he put down his axe and took long strides for the spring yonder, his bare feet, which, like his hands, looked too large for the rest of him, sinking into the soft leaf mold. On hands and knees, he gulped the cool, sweet water and let it trickle down his beardless chin.

He sloshed the sweat from his face, from his ropy muscled arms, and his bony chest, and, as he stood up, he glimpsed in the water his reflected image, which folks along Little Pigeon Creek, in good nature, said was as homely as a scarecrow's. The high cliff of his forehead and the shock of thick black hair, the gray eyes deep in their cave-like sockets under his heavy brows, the angular cheek bones, the firm nose, the large mouth and full under-lip. A gaunt face, a backwoods face, brooding at times.

His sudden smile came. He reckoned that was better than no face a-tall, and a body couldn't help it if he stood a gawky six four at sixteen.

An eagerness started up in him, for his mind was on practicing speeches again. Hurrying back, he pulled on his homespun shirt, and, from the first fork of a young black walnut tree, took down a lop-eared copy of *LESSONS IN ELOCUTION*, found a place in the shade, and dug into his dinner of cornbread and fried salt-pork, reading as he ate, resting on an elbow, his wide mouth puckered in thought, his under-lip protruding.

He didn't know how many times he had read the book, but each time he seemed to husk out new meanings. It said here, under "Elements of Gesture," there were eighty-one "passions and humors." Certain ways to express each one. By jiminy! He'd begin by practicing on pathos.

Soberly mindful of the instructions, he laid the book aside and rose to his gangling length, already feeling self-conscious. He began twisting his mouth this way and that, sideways and slantways; then half shutting his eyes in distress, then opening them wide, lifting his eyebrows and lowering them; resting his right hand over his heart and bowing his head; outstretching one hand in a gesture of succor.

He practiced until his jaws popped, until his eyes felt bugged out of his head. All at once he stopped. Without warning, a little bubble of laughter started rising in him, higher and higher, uncontrolled, until it burst from his throat and he bent over, doubling up chuckling at his awkward efforts. One thing certain, he was no play actor with parlor manners and scrapes and bows. He was a backwoodsman, and he'd better be himself.

He dropped all pretense and became thoughtful, tugging on his chin, scowling. He nodded deliberately, as was his habit, wondering if it wasn't more what you said and how you said it than how you looked when you said it.

Hence, with a hitch at his butternut jeans and a straightening jerk on his shirt, he made a clumsy bow, stationed his feet just so, and faced his forest audience.

"My friends," he said, fast, "I am honored that you would ask me to give my views on internal improvements. May I be pardoned upon this important occasion if, first, I refer to what an old neighbor of ours once said regarding mud holes. . . ." He paused, deciding that he needed to talk slower, not mill-racing his words, and add a neighborly nod there and there, and look straight into the faces of his friends, instead of standing like a stump in a clearing. And so he started over.

"My friends"—nodding all around; that thick oak over there could be his good neighbor, Josiah Crawford; that slender sycamore yonder his tried friend, Allen Gentry, the storekeeper's son—"I hope you will pardon me if, upon this notable occasion, I. . . ."

Once more he stopped himself, remembering that the point of a story should be held to the very last, till you had moved from the head to the tail of it, not spoiled by over-hankering to get it done with, like grubbing stumps. If you didn't hold off, it was a poor make-out of a story.

He nodded to that in his deliberate manner. Which reminded him of a saying he'd thought out, and he stationed himself afresh and spoke in his natural, somewhat high-pitched tone.

"I reckon it's proper for me to reflect a bit on the wages of human labor, scant as they be in these hard times, when a body gets two-bits a day for turnin' out four hundred rails. So

I look at it this way . . . my father raised me to work, but never taught me to love it."

His mind seemed to be turning every which way today, like an old hen caught in the bean patch. His thoughts fanned out to his hero, George Washington, who had returned good for evil, and to the Battle of Trenton, and crossing the ice-clogged river, and the many hardships and the struggle with the Hessians, and Washington riding along the front of his uncertain troops, sword raised, his clear voice rekindling their sagging spirits. "There! My brave friends! There are the enemies of your country! And now, all I ask of you, is just to remember what you are about to fight for. March!"

That memorized passage was seared into his being, and it occurred to him that there must have been something more than common that those men had fought for.

An awareness of passing time tapped him. He had been dreaming and thinking again, which some folks took for laziness, reliving the pages in his worn books. With a glance at the sliding sun, he sighed and skinned off his shirt, picked up his axe, and stepped across to the unfelled oak.

He swung. The flashing blade blurred and chocked. A broad chip flew. He swung faster, making the chips fly as three men might; his neighbors would opine to that as well. The keen pungency of hardwood rose around him as he worked without let-up. After a while, he paused and took a measuring look about; then half-a-dozen quick swings and he heard the first rending crack. The oak swayed and fell crashing—by jiminy!—right where he aimed it to fall, toward an open place, and he felt the trembling jar of the earth's shaken floor.

He set upon the straight trunk in swift strokes, trimming the leafy boughs. Now he laid down the axe and took up a cheese-shaped maul and drove iron wedges into the log to commence the cleavage. Using the wedges, he quartered the halves. Then he gripped the axe and began working up the triangular-shaped rails—about ten feet long, paced off, four inches across, and notched at the ends, which was a kind of trademark of his, to make the ends fit tighter into a snake-rail fence "horse high, bull strong, and pig tight," as the saying went.

As the afternoon wore away and the pile of yellow rails heaped higher, he rested every hour or so to catch his wind, meantime sizing up trees that would make into rails—besides oak, the ash, hickory, poplar, and walnut trees served best.

He wasn't aware that the day was almost gone, spent like a hard-earned coin, until suddenly the blade of his axe blurred before his eyes. He ceased chopping. Holding the axe handle at his side, he swiped a hand across his dripping brow, conscious of the deep hush of dusk. The forest swam with purple shadows. A whippoorwill called, its small voice always somehow sad and mysterious. Suddenly he glanced in that direction, hoping to see its mottled shape, but seldom did a body catch sight of one, and he did not now, like the dreams whose meanings eluded him.

He found his shirt and book, slung the axe over his right shoulder, and struck for home. Before long he came out on what everybody called a road, although it was no better than a beaten trail through the wilderness. Here the light fell stronger. He lengthened stride, thinking of supper.

Behind him he caught the ringing *clop* of a trotting horse. When it sounded near, he turned with a friendly expression, expecting to greet a neighbor.

Instead, he saw a stranger, a thick-set man of middle age astride a blooded sorrel gelding. A town man from his looks, in shiny jackboots, clean gray felt hat, and a handsome dark-green coat. His brown beard hung like a bib down to his chest. He reined up.

"Good evening!" he called.

" 'Evening."

"I trust I'm on the right road to Gentry's store?"

The sudden, obliging smile. "Yes, sir. You're headed just right."

"How far?" There was a weary edge to the gruff voice, and the man had a pecking way of looking at a body, although his eyes were genial enough, if you paid no mind to his air of self-importance.

"About two miles."

"Ah"—the rider expelled a breath of relief—"I'm indeed obliged to you." He clucked to his mount and started past, only to draw rein and look down, a faint suggestion of curious amusement changing his fleshy face. "Boy, you are uncommonly tall, and you've got the biggest and strongest-looking hands I ever saw. What's the family name?"

He'd never been asked that before, in that way, in a community where there were no strangers; and he hesitated, as if his name mattered little. "Most folks back in old Kaintuck called us Linken . . . which I reckon is close enough to sayin' Lincoln, which is what it is."

He saw the rider tuck in his lips, and he saw the faint smile again and afterward the shake of his head, which said the stranger had never heard tell of the name till now, and he saw him ride on.

By jiminy!

He listened to the fading hoof racket, knowing that he came from plain people on both sides of his family, yet thinking that high-sounding names didn't matter a hoot in the wilderness. What counted was what a man was. How he sized up, like a good tree, straight, strong, and true. Not what his ancestors used to be or the kind of stock they owned.

He struck off down the road, taking enormous strides. Tonight after supper he would read near the table until the tallow dip burned low, then he would lie on his back and read until the fire died and his head sagged on his chest and it was time to climb the pegs to his bed in the loft. And like as not he would dream again, for his given name was Abraham.

Beyond the Ridge

Streaky gray showed in the east, and daylight came on. Dave Bonnell stirred in his thin blanket, fully awake at once and listening. He lay there, content to catch the picketed gelding's steady grass-cropping. But presently something like dread traveled through him, and he thought with a running man's misgiving of the day about to begin. He told himself he was a fool to have come back.

Unmoving, he heard the distant *thunking* of the axe across the wooded valley below him, early as usual. It was a noise he had grown to listen for, a small comfort, because it broke the tense monotony of his hidden camp. True, it was an erratic sound, as if the axe-man struck wearily or rested often, yet it was a friendly sound in this watchful world of his. And sometimes on the lifting wind he smelled wood smoke, smoke that made the juices in his mouth run fast.

An insistent hunger was working inside him, and he threw back the blanket. After some moments he stretched his long legs and plowed fingers through his coarse black hair. When he stood up stiffly, a tall man drawn to the lean of his big-boned frame, he sent a sober glance toward his dwindling little mound of supplies. Although deer ran in the thickets, he hadn't dared a meat shot. Now, could he risk one more fire? Only yesterday he had spotted bunched riders in the distance, and they were not moving cattle.

For a long time he stood rooted, rubbing his stubbled jaw. Then, in a rush of desire, his hunger won, and he made a tiny blaze under the overhanging rock by the seep spring. Even after he'd wolfed down the meager breakfast and carefully kicked out the coals, he was still empty. No man, he knew, could keep this up long.

At that moment the thudding of the axe started up again, and he thought of the cabin. Another broad-backed home-steader, he guessed, green to the frontier, staking his future in this cheap, rich land that had been open range for the big out-fits until a year or more ago. In an hour, Dave considered, he could ride down there, buy something, and get back.

He was edging toward the bay horse as he mulled it over. With the picket rope in hand he stopped short, thinking: *I've got to . . . a man's got to eat.* That decided him. Deliberately he saddled up and rode out of the pocket-size clearing into the timber. Before leaving it, farther on along the ridge, he halted and gazed sharply around and beyond. His eyes met a broken, rolling vastness in which nothing stirred among the round-topped hills.

The emptiness satisfied him, and he went ahead, but al-ready the old tight rein of caution held him. His face had a pulled-in feeling, and he wondered if his eyes showed the hunted feeling that had become a part of him in these few days. It was a face normally smooth and untroubled, now grown tight and hollow-eyed.

All this trailed back to the town of Crossroads farther north, to gambler Gib Hambrick falling under the table in the rear of the Drover's House and the acrid smell of blooming powder smoke from the gun in his own knotted hand. Hambrick's bullet had been high and wide. Dave knew the game had been rigged against him and Barney Struck. But that made it no easier for him, for he had shot a man.

There had been the pell-mell ride out of town, with grim Ben Pickett, the federal marshal, hard on their heels. Pickett stuck like a burr until the rough country rose and swallowed them. They bought a few supplies from a nester and rode south for two days. When Barney decided on Texas, Dave had turned back.

Now he became aware of the horse's fidgeting, and he realized he'd been locked in thought again. Instead of dropping down the steep valley trail, he rode west until the uncertain *whacking* of the axe pinched off, until the high-shouldered hills flattened out to a sea of weaving grass, spring green. Afterward he cut a wide half-circle, entered the valley's far end, and crossed Lonesome Creek. All of it was familiar country, so rough as to be shunned by most, which was the reason he had returned to it.

Before him the cabin took shape as a square bulk, hunkered low in the tall timber. Riding closer, he noticed the grayed ends of the notched logs, which told him the cabin's owner was no newcomer. The running walk of the gelding made a rhythmic patter, suddenly loud and carrying in the hacked-out clearing. There was no movement around the place.

Uneasiness touched him, and he reined up. He stared at the feeble pole corral enclosing two bony mules and, drawn up under the trees, a weathered spring wagon that had cast a tire. The almost bare woodpile meant either a lazy man or an absent one. There was a low shed, and its pen had the bars down. Beyond the cabin was a half-grown stand of corn and a struggling garden.

"What d'you want?"

Dave jerked and felt himself flushing. He'd been caught gawking. A woman stood at the cabin's far corner. She held a shotgun uncertainly, as if she had grabbed it up on hearing the sound of his horse.

He touched his floppy hat brim. "Just passing through, ma'am," he said. "I'm low on flour. Can you spare some?"

She tilted her dark head toward the east. "Logan City's ten miles straight over that hill yonder," she told him, making the invitation quite plain.

He saw the fear show like a shadow falling across her face and tenseness of her body, but her tone was level and cool. She was dressed in some kind of loose-fitting gray, the sleeves rolled up to her elbows. Her face was slightly browned and rounded, the full mouth compressed.

"I will pay for the flour." As he spoke, even without insistence, he realized he'd said it wrong.

Suspicion darkened her gray eyes; they told him frankly how rough he must look. She seemed to take a long breath as she pointed the shotgun directly at him. "My husband," she said, after a moment's hesitation, "is nearby. Now, you ride on!"

The abruptness of her fury straightened him. "Sorry, ma'am," he answered, his surprise growing. "No trouble intended." He was reining away when a boy ran from around the cabin to her. Winded and excited, he gave a croupy cough, and Dave noticed his pale, sickly color and felt a sudden pang of regret. He was not more than five or six, with the same large expressive gray eyes as the woman's.

His attention went at once to Dave's bay, to Dave's scarred boots and battered hat, the black gun belt and the holstered saddle gun. In his small boy's expression, wrapped in a sort of dreaming, all Dave's worn gear appeared to take on a wide-eyed magnificence.

"Mama . . . cowboy!" the boy exclaimed, taking a step closer.

She said sharply: "Jimmy, come here." Jerking the boy to her, she swung on Dave. "You get, and don't come back!"

Tight-lipped, he swung the horse back the way he'd ridden in. Angling into the cool woods, he kept thinking of the woman's violent distrust. It was really closer to fear than anything else—the fear of a lonely woman left with a sickly kid. As an afterthought he wondered if she'd been bluffing. And then, seeing again the determined thrust of her rounded face, he decided she wasn't.

Riding on, Dave did not notice the brown shape until brush cracked and the bay horse jumped. A milk cow lifted its motley head, one horn broken.

Dave scanned the thick underbrush, half expecting to see a man following afoot, homesteader style. When nobody appeared after a minute, he moved on. Still the cow lingered, showing no intention of going home, and suddenly Dave found himself remembering the pale-looking boy, maybe a little hungry himself. And there was the small chance, with the cow brought in, that the woman might relent and sell him the flour. Also a chance, he thought wryly, that she might use the shotgun when she saw him coming after ordering him off the place.

Reluctantly he reined and rode straight for the cow. Her head came up, and she lumbered a few paces, then stopped to resume her stubborn grazing. When he urged her forward again, she cut back quickly in the opposite direction. But the bay, liking this old cutting-horse game, instinctively wheeled and headed her. So the cow went a short distance and quit. They moved like that toward the clearing, the cow traveling grudgingly only when Dave pressed in from behind, stopping when he did not.

Dave had his doubts as they made a racket breaking through the brush, loud enough to bring the woman to the door with the boy at her side. She looked straight and formidable with the shotgun in her hands. But her expression

152

showed only relief, mingled with annoyance. She crossed to the milking pen and raised the bars so the cow could enter.

"Guess your husband missed her in the timber," Dave said. "A cowbell would help."

She said nothing, and he turned his horse, feeling his defeat. He had reached the clearing's edge when her even voice came to him.

"Thank you," she said.

Yet, upon bringing his glance around, he saw that her eyes held the same cool distance as before, and the shotgun did not waver. For an instant, as if not quite sure he ought to, the boy gave him a brief wave.

Shadows banked in along the rock ledge, a black curtain behind which the night insects hummed. Dave made pan bread from the last of his flour, then fried bacon and boiled coffee, while he ironed out the decision in his mind. He had to move on, the necessity forced when the woman had refused him flour two days back.

Memory of it stirred his resentment, although faintly, because he could not rightfully blame her. Rough men rode the territory trails these days, most of them like him, running from something. And now that he faced it, he understood why he had hung on, why he hadn't footed on with Barney Struck to Texas, where a man could lose himself forever.

He had to know whether Hambrick lived or had died. Recalling the shooting, Dave figured his bullet had struck high, near the left shoulder. Yet, when in his mind's eye he saw again the man's slack face, he wondered dismally if the shot had entered lower.

After daybreak, he ate breakfast and kicked out the coals of his campfire. On impulse he walked to the low ridge overlooking the valley. It was not time for the chopping sound. He studied the valley, cottony with early haze, and judged where the cabin would be, under its screen of trees. As he watched, delaying his saddling, horsemen bulked below him.

For a moment of white panic Dave stood still. Then hurriedly he flattened out. And he had a sudden knowing, a feeling that comes from hiding, that these men wanted him. He sensed it in the deliberate way they rode, in the searching stares they cast on the rising hills, in the sun flashes on short carbine barrels.

Out in front rode a loose-shouldered man, and even at this distance Dave recognized him. Ben Pickett was so rangy and raw-boned that he loomed a head taller than his companions. On this man Dave kept his eyes because Pickett was always the swinging point of a manhunt.

The riders reined to a tight palavering clump—all but Pickett, who held back, his gaze always busy around him. Only when a posse man gestured westward impatiently did the marshal join them. His wide-brimmed hat bobbed as he talked. There was no more gesturing. In a moment they swung north and put their mounts to the sloping, rocky trail.

Dave's mouth was dry. He watched them come on, feeling the trembling quakiness in his stomach. He had slipped out his pistol, but did not remember reaching for it. Now the posse was so close below him, strung out single file, that he could see Pickett's drooping mustaches. Realization was a wave rolling and flooding his mind, telling him that they had passed the cabin. Had the woman told them?

But the thought spun away, and his attention was pinned again on Pickett, who had halted in front. He was taking a long time for his look-see, Dave knew. With the interest of a cat-eyed man he must be seeing things that escaped ordinary men. Dread grew on Dave, and the waiting became worse. A turn to the right now, off the seldom used trail and along the high ground of the ridge, would expose his camping place.

He drew in his breath, expelled it slowly when Pickett touched spurs and went on over the hill. Raw relief warmed Dave, and he waited a long time, long after the distant ring of shod hoofs on loose rock had run out. Not until then did he push up and flex his stiff muscles.

As he straightened, the far-off thudding of axe against wood came clearly, broken in rhythm. He thought of the woman and the boy, but dismissed the image for another of Texas to the south and west.

Soon afterward he left the camp and jogged west, looking carefully, intending to avoid the valley. He passed through the last of the timber, and the open spaces seemed to beckon and wave him onward. Ahead of him grazed a lone cow. He scarcely paid it notice at first. Approaching it, however, he felt first a beginning recognition and next a twinge of annoyance.

There was no mistaking the motley head and the broken horn. It was the woman's stubborn cow, wandered from the valley for this rich grass. She was like a human, almost, figuring it to be better over the ridge and where she hadn't been before.

Irritation piled up in Dave, a disgust for homesteaders who knew nothing about keeping up stock. The woman, in his judgment, would not think to search this far. She couldn't, with the boy at her heels. Dave disregarded the man, because a man who did not bell a cow in rough country was a poor stockman.

Haste urged him on. Yet, even as he circled the cow, turning her, he knew that he was risking a chance if the posse came back.

An hour later he saw the cabin, and the woman was out in front. She dropped the axe at once and took up the shotgun leaning against the cabin wall.

As the cow ambled past her into the pen, the woman said: "She broke out last night."

Uncomfortable before the shotgun, Dave said with an attempt at good humor: "You can put that down. I'm traveling."

"You were passing through the other day." She put a certain emphasis on the *passing,* and there was skepticism in her tone, and distrust. She appeared drawn, which gave Dave the impression that she had an inner concern, detached and apart from him. "All kinds of men ride by here. Today there was a posse. Mister Pickett, the federal marshal, has set up headquarters at Logan City. He's looking for a man." Her eyes, changing expression, searched his face briefly.

"Country's full of rough men," agreed Dave, and he smiled down at her, seeking to give her the confidence he thought she needed. "Good thing your husband. . . ."

From inside the cabin came a boy's cough, drawn-out and ragged. Like a flash the woman turned. She hurried inside, and Dave heard her talking, her voice soothing. When she returned to the door, worry etched tiny lines around the corners of her eyes. But she still held the gun on him.

"You got a sick boy?" asked Dave.

She barely nodded, and he saw the fixed expression, deep in the eyes, like a fear she was trying to hide before a stranger. Dave's roaming glance settled on the woodpile. As usual, it looked scant.

A puzzled anger stirred in him, and he forced down the desire to ask about her husband. Instead he said, "I'm in no big hurry, and you need wood." Hardly aware of his intent, he swung down and tramped across to the woodpile. There was a chopping block and little else.

"I will cut my own wood," she told him, a ring of pride in her voice.

"Ma'am," he said, "this stuff wouldn't make fire for coffee." His impatience grew, and he picked up the axe and went forward in his cowman's choppy gait to the timber. Searching, he found a short oak sapling and slashed it down. He dragged it back to the yard, threw it across the chopping block, and began swinging. His gun belt felt cumbersome, and after a while he unbuckled it and laid it aside. When he had cut the sapling into stove lengths, he gathered up the short chunks and faced her. "I'll take this in," he said, waiting.

She hesitated, her eyes reading him again. "All right," she said.

He walked past her into the cabin. He saw the wood box by the black stove and dropped his load. At the noisy thumping he made, he remembered the boy and turned. The boy lay on a crude bunk, flush-faced and hollowy eyed, covered with quilts.

"Guess I woke you up," Dave said regretfully.

The boy managed a faint grin, but he shook his head weakly. His round eyes centered on Dave, interested and puzzled. "Your six-shooter . . . where is it?" There was no strength in his voice, only a strained and ragged huskiness.

"Why," said Dave, "I left it outside." He was suddenly awkward before the sick boy, with nothing helpful to say.

Dave saw the woman soberly watching the young face. The boy coughed again, the sound coming from deep down, and she touched his forehead. Standing there, Dave was conscious of a stranger's clumsiness. He shifted in his boots and glanced around the neat room. There was a double bunk, a cupboard, a rough table, and some chairs. All at once he was struck by the bareness, bare even for this rough land where luxuries were few, and he felt a shameful regret about asking for the flour.

"Well," he said, "I'll get along now."

Almost mechanically she answered: "I'm obliged to you." But she still held the shotgun, and her eyes were straight on him.

Her boy stirred uneasily, his eyes on Dave, and Dave gave him a grin and went outside. Buckling on the gun belt, he snapped a look back at her in the doorway, arrested by a sudden thought. "There's a doctor in Logan City. Your husband. . . ." He did not finish.

Although he could not tell for certain, he thought her mouth trembled slightly. She was on the verge of telling him something. Then, slowly, she straightened her slim shoulders, and her dark head came up. "Jimmy's a little better this morning," she said. Her tone lacked conviction.

He did not press the question, and her eyes told him nothing. He was silently reminding himself that this was none of his worry and in another hour he'd be traveling open country. Somehow, though, try as he might, he wasn't thinking so much about Texas. His mind was a free thing over which he had no control, that drifted back to what he'd seen in the cabin—its overwhelming impression of hard times— the sick boy and the man always gone when needed. An old story, Dave realized, his cowman's contempt rising. Homesteaders pushed out to the frontier's edge, unprepared for the land's demands. Many of them were good dirt farmers, but many were unequal to the task and poor providers.

His protest growing, he walked quickly to the gelding and jerked the carbine from the boot. As he heeled around, she demanded suspiciously: "What're you doing?"

"Going hunting. Still plenty of time to ride."

"There's no call for you . . . ," she began.

He was gone into the dark timber before she could finish.

In the late afternoon he returned, bent forward under a young buck slung over his shoulder. His luck had held. He had bagged the deer with only one shot, and the angle tricky. And he'd waited long after the echo thinned out before he went over. Coming back, he'd stayed to the woods as best he could. In him, now, he could feel the haste hammering for him to ride on.

Grunting wearily, he dropped the deer. It made a racket that brought her to the door. "How's the boy?" he asked quietly, and, as he spoke, he heard the broken cough inside. He noticed that her hands were empty.

"I . . . I don't know." Her gaze slid away from him, returned when he drew a handful of stubby roots from his pocket.

She stared down. "What's that?"

"Red root," he said. "You boil it. Makes a strong tea with sugar. Might help him, loosen him up inside."

Urgency threaded all through him as she took the roots inside, for he knew it was past time to go. He had lingered here long enough, maybe too long. Quickly he cleaned and quartered the venison and hung it in the fork of a tree, wrapped in his yellow saddle slicker. He was washing up at the bench outside the cabin, frowning over the labored coughing of the boy, when he heard the abrupt rush of her feet across the floor. She appeared suddenly in the doorway, and he knew without asking.

"He's . . . he's worse," she said, and covered her face with her hands.

Dave ducked inside the low-roofed room, his glance narrowing on the bunk. The boy looked even paler than he had a few hours before. His eyes were closed, and Dave could hear his tortured breathing plainly. Fear hit him like a blow as he turned away, dogged by the sense of wrongness about this place, this family, by a feeling that he ought not leave.

He took her arm, led her outside. "Look here, ma'am," Dave said gravely, "you mentioned your husband. Can't he go into town for a doctor? He can get Doc Harvey, I know. And he's good with kids."

Her eyes avoided his, and he went on, surprised when he heard the roughness of his voice. "Where is he?"

She had been quietly crying. But in a moment she looked up, and he could feel the strong pride bracing her. Her eyes seemed to bore right through him, fighting an inner, silent struggle. It came to him that he still gripped her arm, so he dropped his hand.

"My husband," she said in an odd, squeezed-out voice, "died a year ago." And this, he recognized, was what she'd been holding back. "We came out here from Missouri. Land was high back home and he said we'd have a better chance in the territory. He always figured a homestead would be something for Jimmy when he grew up. Well, I'm Jessie Overby . . ."—there was the faintest break in her voice—"and I've tried to work the place. But I'm afraid I'm not much of a farmer."

For long moments Dave stood with lowered head, a hard-muscled man turned awkward and stiff and not knowing what to say next. Finally he said: "You've got neighbors?" He knew—and damned it—that his hope climbed like a signal on his face.

It drifted away as she shook her head, uncertain again. "Nobody close. Dry weather burned most folks out last year. One family still lives five, six miles west. But nobody I know. We've stuck close."

Dave considered this impassively, figuring the distance

west and back. Too great now. Logan City to the east. If he found a homesteader, likely it'd be one with a slow-footed horse. His thoughts circled again, came back, and settled. He pulled in a long breath, and a soberness caught him. There was a gap of silence, running on, so still that he could hear her breathing close beside him.

Realization flicked distantly, formed with a surprising clarity, solid and sure, as it marched across his mind. It had been there all the time. In a voice so low and strange that it seemed to come from a great distance, he said: "The bay horse can travel."

Her eyes widened, searching his face, as if seeing him fully for the first time—his sun-burned features dark as an Indian's, the lean frame, the worn shirt and Levi's and the scuffed boots.

Without a word, he left her and mounted. Reining around, he took one backward glance. She hadn't moved. Her eyes met his. "You know the way?" she asked.

"Yes, ma'am. I know Logan City."

Then he touched spurs, and the lazy shoulder muscles were bunching under him. He wondered why she hadn't come right out and asked him to go. On the heels of that he guessed he understood why: it was her pride that had kept her here when the others around her had packed up.

Eastward the land rose and fell, dark timber and high hills and patches of prairie, up-and-down country with rocky ridges. He found a faint trail and rode hard along it until the bay slackened, so Dave eased up and let the gelding blow. Presently they ran on again, pounding a trail that grew wider, and gradually the roughness smoothed out of the land, and they followed a wagon road.

It was early evening when he sighted Logan City, a cluster of yellow lights blinking like fireflies on the flat prairie.

Caution ran through him, cool as the lifting wind, as he entered the street, quiet at this hour. He tied up at the first hitching post and went forward afoot. He kept looking for Ben Pickett's tall figure. Doc Harvey's office and sleeping quarters, he remembered, were over Duren's Saddle Shop in the center of town. He found it and quietly climbed the narrow stairs.

There was no light under the door. But Harvey, a busy man, slept whenever he could. Dave pounded loudly, again and again. After a time he came down to the street, all his dread rising.

A man tramped by on the plank walk. From deep in the shadows Dave asked: "Where's Doc Harvey tonight?"

"Over at Mills's store, talking politics as usual," came the answer. The townsman turned curiously before going on.

Reluctance filled Dave, a holding back. He forced himself down the street, trying to appear casual. Light burned in Mills's General Store, and Dave paused and looked in. Harvey, his back turned, stood talking while Frank Mills, who was closing for the night, tallied his books. Harvey's black medicine bag lay on the counter.

There was a coolness along Dave's neck as he stepped inside. He was coming up behind Harvey when Mills, a stout, puffy man of middle age with nervous hands, glanced up irritably over square-lensed glasses. Recognition flared across his round face. He swallowed in surprise, and Dave saw the instant fear. Doc Harvey had caught the expression and turned.

"Doc," said Dave, rougher than he intended, "a homesteader's kid's sick out on Lonesome Creek. Pneumonia, maybe. Come on."

Instinctively Harvey reached for the bag. Then he hesitated and drew back, all at once thoughtful. "Well, Dave," he said. A kind of curious speculation kindled the tired eyes, not the jumpy fear that shone in Mills's face. He was an overly lank man, pale and unkempt and slow-moving, his face set in a perpetually patient look.

"Come on!" Dave's voice rang with impatience. "It's a rough country. I'll have to show you."

Doc Harvey nodded wearily, and the haggardness crept across his cheeks again. He straightened as if to go.

"No, Doc." Mills had to push back from the counter, both plump hands braced against it. His small black eyes bulged, and he flung his suspicion at Harvey. "Don't you see it? Barney Struck's out there in the hills, shot up. This is for him. There's no kid!"

Sickness came over Dave, a feeling of lost time. He said hoarsely: "Stay out of this."

He thought he'd won then, just for a moment, because Harvey picked up the bag, and Mills seemed to freeze. But the thing Dave had feared broke before him in a wild and crazy swiftness. Mills bent and dug under the counter, then his hand came whipping up. With the shine of the pistol a dim flicker in his eyes, Dave lunged and struck Mills along the jaw. The sound was flat and powerful in the room. Mills's head rolled; he lost the gun and fell backward on the floor. He fell heavily and did not get up.

Dave heaved around with his own pistol swinging, expecting anything.

Doc Harvey's face was unreadable. "I guess," he said, "it was hit or be shot. Nevertheless, I don't like this. Now where's Struck?" He was not a big man physically, yet in that moment he seemed to grow larger. His gaze held level, unwavering; it demanded the truth.

"In Texas," said Dave, and deliberately holstered his pistol.

163

After a moment Harvey growled: "All right. Of course, I'd go even it were Struck, y'understand, but I won't have you lying to me. If Pickett sees you. . . ." He left it unfinished. Already he was striding for the door.

They stepped outside the streaky dark of the street, where scattered horsemen jogged past. At a fast walk they reached the livery stable. Harvey called for two fresh horses. Mounted up, Dave thought with regret of the bay left behind. It was a better horse, he judged, than the one he rode.

They heard the first shout, hoarse on the wind, as they loped out of town. Heading into the darkness, Dave understood dismally how it all must look: Dave Bonnell, who had shot one man, had beaten Frank Mills and kidnapped Doc Harvey to doctor his pard.

He shivered not from coldness but because there seemed no way out of this. Once, when they pulled up to listen, he asked Doc Harvey: "Is Gib Hambrick still alive?"

"Just came in tonight. Been fighting measles the last two days down at the railroad camp."

Faint hoof beats sounded behind them, coming as a far-off roll of drums. They came closer, and Dave went angling off the trail. He knew this country as only a man could who had combed cattle from the scrubby timber and the long-running hills. They rode by sense, by feel, until finally Dave said: "Over there." He'd have found the cabin, he thought, even without the light.

In the yard, Doc Harvey dismounted heavily and tramped to the door. Jessie Overby waited there, and Dave saw where she had nail-hooked a lantern for them. As Harvey hurried inside, Dave saw her turn with him, the light pale on her face. A fine-looking woman, he thought, and mighty brave. Then he tied the horses and stood outside a moment, reluctant to go, afraid of what he might see. But he forced the feeling down and made himself enter.

There was a coal-oil lamp burning. Doc Harvey turned from the bunk, his low voice matter-of-fact. "Dave . . . a good fire . . . hot water." Jessie Overby's eyes never strayed from the bunk. Her face told Dave that her entire life lay there before her.

Dave moved, and it was pure relief no longer to be standing still with his mind numb, feeling helpless. He cut shavings and started a fire from the short saplings left in the wood box. Afterward he took the lantern and axe and prowled the timber, and came back with all the wood he could drag. This he cut with long, powerful strokes, until he had an armful. When he carried it to the cabin, Harvey and Jessie Overby had not stirred from the bunk. Dave returned to the woodpile. He drove the axe savagely, as if by doing so he could smash the quiet terror inside the still cabin.

Long afterward, he went dead-footed to the doorway. The moment he slumped down to rest, it swarmed over him—all the hard riding and stomach emptiness and punishing pressures of this night and the nights and the days before. He heard voices murmuring from the other side of that distant world where Doc Harvey waged his patient fight.

Dave glanced up at the sky and saw it was near light, brushing daybreak. He was suddenly startled, for he'd dozed off. His mind whipped the warning at him—*Ride while you can.* Somewhere in the slow-breaking light, in the timber and brush, a posse prowled. He stood up and felt the ache tight in his shoulders and arms. What if he left now? Could he ride away and never know about the boy? *Why,* he thought, *it was like needing to know about Hambrick, the gambler, only stronger.*

Sound, so faint he hardly noticed it at first, drifted out of the smoky grayness blanketing the clearing. Old danger signals came bristling. Dave felt the knot in the pit of his stomach. Voices grew in the cabin.

"Dave." Doc Harvey stood close behind him, and abruptly Dave was fearful of what the doctor had to say. He half turned, his attention reaching out to the padding sound in the timber.

Dave's mouth turned dry. He hated to face Doc Harvey, and he couldn't take his eyes off the timber. He started to speak, but he never got it out.

Horses filled the clearing in violent motion, striking across it toward the cabin, and he sensed that he was too late as he straightened and faced them. Now riders bunched before him. His hand brushed his holster, then dropped away. He just stood there, wondering why he made no effort to lift his pistol.

"Come out, Bonnell!" It was a tall man on a swerving horse.

Arms loose and hanging, Dave stepped slowly out. Riders closed in at once, while others slammed in behind the cabin. He thought: *They figure Barney's running out the back.* He looked up into the shifting muzzles of carbines and pistols. The tall man loomed over him. He recognized grim Ben Pickett, hard as nails, drooping mustaches making his iron-jaw face still sharper.

Pickett split his hard gaze between Dave and the cabin. "Barney Struck in there?" he demanded.

An overwhelming weariness hit Dave, and he shook his head. He knew Pickett didn't believe him.

It was Doc Harvey who spoke up next, talking as he walked forward, his manner severe. "Pickett," he said curtly, "you're kicking up a pack of noise with a sick boy inside. Struck isn't here . . . never has been. Dave didn't have to ride into town to get me, but he did. Y'understand that? And Mills, the meddling fool, almost stopped him." Then Doc

Harvey completely ignored the marshal and the posse-men. "As I was about to say, Dave, when they came up . . . give me your six-shooter. Orders from the sick room. We got a patient on the mend, and I never like to disappoint a boy."

The lifting meaning traveled through Dave suddenly, like summer heat lightning. He unbuckled the gun belt, handed it over, and faced Pickett with the question leaping in his mind. "Hambrick," he said. "What about him?"

The marshal blew on his thorny mustaches. "Gib Hambrick," he began, and paused, "will live to be ninety if he quits cards. Frank Mills has a sore head. It's my opinion that a man ought to leave regulating to the proper authorities." His voice lacked its usual bite as he finished. "But we'll have to take you in."

It was time to go. Dave wondered if a man never stopped riding. He was up and mounted when he noticed Jessie Overby standing in the doorway. He guessed she'd heard it all.

He glanced uneasily at Pickett, who still dallied, held by the same sight. She was, Dave decided, a woman of strong mind, and yet she could be pliant or stormy, all a man hoped for.

Then she moved, not away from him but almost running across the yard. In a moment she stood at his stirrup. She seemed years younger, her face rounded and with an expression he'd never seen there before. He wondered if his admiration showed, but he didn't care, for he wanted her to see it.

"This is our man, Dave Bonnell," Ben Pickett said, although not seeming proud of it. He went on curiously: "Missus Overby, you didn't tell us he was around the other day, when we stopped here."

She looked long at Pickett. "He wasn't here." Yet there was no defiance in her voice, just the gentleness of a woman, often alone, who maybe noticed things a man never saw even in himself.

Grim Ben Pickett made no answer. But he did a gallant thing. He touched hand to hat brim in salute.

Then she turned, and Dave saw her eyes, squarely upon him, silently thanking him. "That's why I couldn't ask you to go in town," she told him. "I knew what it meant, but I guess I knew you would go. Dave, you'll come back, after all this is over."

Dave Bonnell nodded. It was the most certain thing of his life, and he was still hearing the magic of his name as she had spoken it. She had said that he would come back, and he knew it was sure to come, something deep down telling him so. Now, riding off with the others at Pickett's gruff command, he decided that was more than enough to carry a man through the days ahead, whatever they held for him. It was good to think about.

Gunfighter's Choice

Sometimes the solitary feeling pushed a man hard, drove him against his better judgment. Jeff Cole's excuse to himself was the need of a drink. But jogging into Spur, he knew that his real hunger was for company, the drawling, friendly talk of men. He wanted to ride leisurely along Main Street, with his head up, without that cold twinge at the base of his spine.

Tying up in front of the Texas House, he noticed heads turning. How long, he thought soberly, before the word fanned through town that the owlhoot, Jeff Cole, was back? He looked up as two 'punchers jangled into the saloon. They were a thin-faced boy with a slight swagger to his high-heeled walk, and an older, chunky rider. Too young to remember, Jeff figured, glancing along the grit-whipped street.

It almost gave him a start to see the spare, loose-jointed shape of Jim Banning, the town marshal, prowling the boardwalk again. Jeff tabbed him for a talk later, and stepped inside. With something like hunger he breathed in the damp, stale smell. The light was shadowed, and he blinked.

There was a card game slapping in the back corner and the two 'punchers stood slouched against the bar. Jeff read them at a glance—well-heeled, two guns apiece swung low—and he felt a vague caution. You could spot them like bulls in a heifer pen. He went to the bar and called for whisky. When the bottle was brought him, he poured a drink. He eyed it morosely, feeling his depression.

Catching his reflection in the huge back mirror that ran the bar's length, he stared in critical appraisal. He had been a youth when he'd fled to Mexico, chased by a posse, following that shooting scrape. Now he saw a gaunt man, wind-burned, the eye corners squint-lined in the square, leather-brown face. At thirty-four Jeff Cole was showing the strain of traveling the lonesome places, sleeping in thin blankets, eating like a coyote.

Jaw tight, Jeff looked away. He was making idle circles on the polished wood with the bottom of his glass when he heard the barkeep's low mutter. When Jeff glanced up, the man was staring, recognition in the mild, hound-brown eyes. He was squatty and bald, with a friendly, fat-rolled face. Jeff's mind clicked, searching for a name—Bill Higgins. The years had broadened him, but Jeff remembered.

"You. . . ." Higgins' voice was wondering. "Jeff, you're back!"

Frowning, Jeff nodded, and he knew that the 'punchers had heard by the way they jerked.

"No need to spread it around," Jeff said. "I don't want any more trouble. Everybody will hear soon enough."

"Why, you bet, Jeff. Sure. . . ." Abruptly the fat man was wiping the spotless bar with nervous motions, his round face white, strained. "Glad to see you. If you need anything . . . you did me a good turn, once. Let me see . . . been about eleven years, I guess."

You just did me a poor turn, Jeff thought bleakly, speaking out. It had been longer than eleven years. More like ten lifetimes.

The drink had gone bitter, and Jeff realized that he should have known better. People didn't forget. Despite the passage of time, you still carried the stamp, and riding in here was asking for it. But he knew that he couldn't put it off forever, this coming back to Spur to start over again where it had all started. He had shot his first gun-fanner here. A blustering, wild-eyed badman, just come up the Goodnight Trail, looking for trouble, and Jeff hadn't backed down.

He guessed now that had been his trouble all along, the stubbornness, the stiff pride. But he had left more than a clean name behind him. Delia and Cathy lived here. Taking a step, Jeff wondered what they looked like.

"Hey, you!"

Startled, Jeff wheeled as he caught the challenging tone. It hit him that this was the start of the hard, brittle pattern again. You moved to new country, worked till somebody raked up the owlhoot past. Or till some gun-happy hand crawled you. Then you shot a man and rode off. Jeff Cole wasn't a wanted man any more, but as a gunfighter he might as well have been. It was the name. The one-notch boys— such as the slim kid and his blocky partner sliding along the bar now—yearned to add his name to their list and bolster their reps.

"Have a drink?" It was the younger rider talking.

Jeff looked them over. There was a reckless glitter in the kid's clear blue eyes. But the other one was the dangerous man. His head was too small for the thick shoulders, Jeff noticed through long habit, and the narrow-spaced eyes were red and bleary in a flat-nosed face.

"Much obliged," Jeff said tonelessly. "But I've had mine." He was turning when the broad-chested man flanking the kid muttered darkly, and Jeff froze. He had the closed-in feeling of trying to avoid trouble, of failing miserably. The big fellow was weaving, teetering on his boot heels.

"We heard," he grunted in a thick tone. "Maybe our whisky ain't good enough for you."

From the rim of his eye, Jeff caught Higgins's frantic arm-waving meant for the 'punchers. "Thanks, Bill," Jeff said coldly, "but that Kansas City mirror won't get busted by me. I wouldn't waste the lead on these peckerwoods." His half-emptied whisky glass was still on the bar, and he gripped it. For an instant he held it, staring and reluctant.

He took a deep breath. Then with a sweeping swing of his arm, he threw the whisky at the beefy, challenging face of the rider. There was a flat splat. Flustered, the man pawed at his mouth. He lunged forward with both arms raised, but Jeff hit him before he got them fully up. He smashed the long jaw with a short hook that made a sodden *thunk* in the room. As the thick face tilted back, Jeff drove a fist above the wide gun belt. His man doubled up, calling harshly to the kid.

"Get him! Get him!"

There was murder in the hoarse voice, and Jeff swung around. "Don't move," he snapped.

The boy hesitated, eyes traveling from his downed partner back to Jeff.

"Go on . . . make him draw!"

The shoot-out was coming, Jeff sensed, and in an instant it came to him with a shock that his gamble had failed. Instead of sidetracking trouble, his fists had only touched off the inevitable gun play. He saw the blue eyes widen, the young mouth compressing with a reckless purpose, a fighter's pride in his irons. Then the kid's glance lifted, and Jeff heard boots pounding behind him.

"Break it up!"

Risking a cautious glance, Jeff saw Jim Banning stride to a spraddle-legged halt. Wrinkled hands hung on his gun belt, thumbs hooked over the brass-topped cartridges. Jeff saw recognition flare in the faded, smoky-gray eyes.

"You stir things up quick, Jeff," he said critically.

"He didn't start it!" It was Higgins's outraged voice breaking in. "Ed Blanchard tried to bulldoze Jeff into drinking with him."

Loose, deliberate, Banning sauntered forward. "Never mind who," he drawled, slanting his head toward the street. "You Blanchard boys clear out. Jeff, you better come along." He looked at the kid gunman, a question in his eyes. "Dave, you're bitin' off a big chunk. This man's quick . . . out of your class in a shootin' match."

Dave Blanchard's face flamed, and his slender body grew rigid. Behind him, Jeff saw Ed Blanchard on his feet, rubbing his jaw.

"Owlhooters ain't so tough," young Blanchard growled recklessly, and he wheeled, facing Jeff. "Next time you better come loaded."

Jeff shrugged, watching the pair start out at a reluctant walk. Banning turned, and Jeff followed. Outside, he saw the Blanchards mount and ride off at a hard lope.

"They'd like to be tough," Banning shook his head regretfully. "Now, Dave, there, is kind of like you were once. Not mean, but Ed eggs him on, and he won't back down. I guess pride's filled half of Boot Hill."

Down the street a woman walked from a store. She turned this way with a swinging step, a bundle under her arm. Something about her caught Jeff's eye. Something balled up tight inside him, an odd panic. It was Delia, a matured woman now, but slim and dark and not showing the years. Distantly he heard Banning's apologetic murmur: "See you later." Banning crossed to the other side of the street.

Jeff walked to meet Delia. He fumbled with his brush-beaten, brim-flopped hat, feeling the awkward silence. He searched her face. For a second he saw a faint expression there that he couldn't define. Slowly a firm graveness slid across her features. The cool gray eyes and the set of the full mouth told him there was nothing there for him.

"I heard you were back." She spoke in a low, matter-of-fact way that sobered him, chilling him. For he'd had his dim, unreasoning hopes. "You look worn-out, almost ragged." Her straight glance was on the torn shirt pocket, censoring him for his unkempt, drifter-marked appearance. Her fingers strayed almost to the pocket, hesitated, and fell away.

"It's been a long time," he managed to say.

"They vindicated you in regard to that killing," she said severely, "but you didn't come back." Her eyes condemned him, the soft lines of her face unforgiving, hard. "You didn't have to stay away."

"Too late . . . a man who's been on the dodge, with a gunfighter's name, is dragging you down. . . ." He was stumbling for words with the realization that their talk was circling, getting nowhere. "I don't blame you," he said in a half swallowed bitterness. "I had nothing to offer. I sent what money I could."

She seemed to shrink back, and Jeff, knowing that he had said the wrong thing, saw the pent-up resentment, the livid hurt like the lash of a quirt. She gave him a long, raking glance, and then her slim shoulders dropped.

"I . . . I wasn't going to tell you." She was looking away from him deliberately. "You don't deserve to know, and I won't tell her you're here. But Cathy is getting married soon." Delia paused, and Jeff noticed the fine tracery of worry in the wide-spaced eyes. "You don't know the young man. He's wild, but a good boy."

Her voice was more of a hope, a determined apology, as she stepped away. He was staring after her, awkwardly gripping the grimy hat, fighting a growing realization. It cut into him like a knife that she didn't want him here. Not that he had expected more, yet it hurt and twisted him, deep down. But he hadn't told her what was really in his mind—that he had come back to start over again. Another thought, smarting to his pride, was how Delia had managed for them. For he knew that his letters with money, sent when he had it, hadn't provided enough. He was still watching Delia when she turned in at a high-fronted building. Then he saw the lettering on the window: **Delia Cole's Dress Shop**.

His boots beat a slow, booming echo on the walk as he went, slow-footed, to his gelding. He climbed into the saddle, rode to the feed barn, came back up the street, and registered at the hotel. In his room, when he had washed and shaved, he felt some of the bone-weariness leave. There wasn't another shirt in his blanket roll, so he shrugged into the old one again, remembering Delia's critical eyes. It rolled through him somberly that the torn pocket pretty well showed what he was—a man too hard and gone too long, a drifter loose on the hot wind. It was like Delia, he decided, to notice little things that dug into his pride.

When he went downstairs and crossed to the courthouse, Jim Banning was waiting, his boots propped high on the spur-scarred desk. Banning ran skinny fingers through his bone-white hair.

"Guess you want my guns," Jeff said.

Banning grunted and shifted his lanky body with the weariness of a cowman who'd never accustomed himself to the footwork of tramping Spur's dusty streets. "Nope," he said slowly, bushy eyebrows lifting, "you might need 'em."

"Meaning?"

"That the Blanchard boys will be back. You'll have to shoot or pull out of town."

Jeff felt himself growing rigid. "I don't want any trouble," he said. "I came to stay this time." In his own mind he'd known that somehow it would shake around to this.

"You'll have to choose." The marshal was staring thoughtfully at the reward notices tacked in aimless pattern on the wall. "But if you build some smoke, I'll have to take you in. This town has tamed down a lot, Jeff. No trail herds through here any more. People go to church and nesters come in wagons."

"Tell that to the Blanchards," Jeff snapped. "They don't seem to know." Irritated, he got up, but the older man paid no attention.

"I don't understand it all." Banning might have been talking to himself, his muttering voice sounded so slow and deliberate. "Ed and Dave aren't blood brothers. Old Tom Blanchard, who moved in after you left, took Ed in when he was just a nubbin, and gave him a name. But when Tom died, he left the ranch to Dave. Funny way to do things. They're both wild, but Ed's got the mean streak. He's older, too. I figure Dave'll settle down in time."

Jeff was looking at the seamed, wrinkled face. "What if something happened to Dave?"

The marshal's gray head jerked. "Why, the ranch would go to Ed." Abruptly he pulled down his boots and stood up, gape-mouthed. *"Say!"*

Jeff was already at the door. "Figure it out for yourself," he rapped harshly. "But no gun-crazy kid is going to run me out."

"Hold on, Jeff." Banning was swinging around the desk. "Didn't Delia tell you about Cathy?"

"Yeah." Jeff couldn't force down the hoarse sarcasm. "And maybe you think I should give her away. Down at the church you talked about. That's a good one." He was striding through the door when he heard Banning's voice, high and sharp.

"You . . . you damned fool . . . she's marryin' Dave Blanchard!"

Jeff jerked, froze. He stood very still, slowly straightening. Something sick churned in his stomach, and then he was outside, with the almost pleading voice drumming in his ears. Decision was strong in his mind as he paced to the hotel steps. But Jeff Cole had never run, he told himself. Never! A man had his pride. He looked down the street and felt a sudden urge to go on to the dress shop. Yet if he saw her, he knew that they'd only talk again in the same aimless, hurting circles. Deliberately he turned and walked inside.

After supper he sat on the long front porch, back in the shadows, and smoked till the street's traffic slackened and died and the yellow fingers of light spilling from the Texas House finally snapped out. The street was dark, with the hot wind rising and moaning, when he tramped upstairs.

It was a bleak, gusty world of grit and wind when he came down for breakfast. Afterward, from his place on the porch, he saw Delia and a girl move along the street on the far side. Delia walked with her head straight, set, not looking his way. Jeff didn't have to tell himself that the girl was Cathy, although he hadn't seen her in ten years now. She was Delia at eighteen, with the same slimness, the same head-turning darkness, the same light swing to her walk. Watching them disappear in a store, he had a left out feeling.

When Jim Banning limped over in his sore-footed way from the courthouse, there was a question close to the surface in the mild eyes as he looked up and halted.

"Fine day for ridin'," he observed. "Poor day for sittin'."

The invitation was plain enough, but Jeff shook his head. "I'll take the sitting," he said with a flat refusal. "Maybe I'll look for a job. Maybe I'll just sit here and watch Spur ride by.

But I won't run. If the Blanchards come helling, I'll be here. Could be they'll back out."

"They won't."

"Damned if I'll run."

"I was afraid of that." Banning spread his bony hands wide and shrugged his slack shoulders. "Still a good day for traveling." Then he moved down the street, wearily starting his rounds.

Doubt knotted up inside Jeff, a reminder of his hardheadedness. He turned it over in his mind. It would be easier all around if he just rode off, left Spur as it was. He was thinking about it when he saw dust streaks clouding the road into town. Two men were riding at a steady trot, and suddenly Jeff knew, even before he could make out the riders.

He saw them ride onto Main Street. Something grew cold within him, and he got up slowly, carefully. Reason told him that it was two against one. And he felt a reluctance, a hesitation, as he stepped inside and turned to watch. Almost casually they rode past the Texas House. Dave Blanchard had an easy looseness with his swagger, a reckless look in his swinging glance. Ed Blanchard was heavy in the saddle, flat-nosed face slanted down, beady eyes searching the street.

They pulled up once, looking. Jeff couldn't hear them, but he saw the rapid working of young Blanchard's jaws in a hard-imaged face, and the sullen expression of Ed Blanchard didn't change. They rode on, and Jeff was aware of a cool sweat breaking over him. He couldn't run, he kept telling himself with a surge of the old pride. He didn't want to run.

Grim, he was standing stiff-legged as Cathy walked out of the store. She shaded her eyes against the sun. Her face changed with a quick, pleased expectancy when Dave Blanchard swung toward her. Their glances met, held level, till Ed Blanchard's thick lips moved. Jeff caught the unwilling, laggard lift of the boy's rein hand. The same awareness that Jeff had sensed in the saloon flashed over him—Ed Blanchard was the troublemaker, the one to watch. Cathy's eyes were puzzled, hurt. She was looking after them as the brothers pointed their horses down street. Jeff couldn't take his eyes off the girl. He was seeing her doubt and bewilderment, her troubled, small-girl face.

He was swinging away, half up the protesting board steps of the lobby, before he realized what he was about to do. Jeff Cole, the gunfighter who had never backed down, was running from a fight. He hurried to his cramped room, rolled up the thin blanket. Downstairs, he left a dollar at the clerk's empty desk, took a quick glance at the street. The Blanchards had gone. Out in front, Delia had joined Cathy.

Relief ran through him, relief and regret. He took them in with one long glance, the slim woman and the dark-eyed, pretty girl. Then he was wheeling down the long hall that opened on the back entrance. At the door, he looked both ways, stepped to the alley. His spurs made a jingling discord as he ran to the livery stable. There was a pole corral in back, closing in half a dozen horses, but Jeff's animal wasn't there. He climbed up, jumped down, and headed for the dark opening of the barn. It was quiet, he realized, almost too quiet. He heard the muffled stamping from the stalls, the rustle of muzzles nosing hay.

Stepping inside, he could hear his own ragged breathing. The dank smell of horses was strong. Gradually his eyes adjusted to the near-darkness. Down the runway he could pick out the rumps of haltered animals. He saw his gelding quartered near the front, close by the stable office where the light broke the gloom. His heart was slugging a drumbeat in his chest when he went forward.

Long-striding, he reached the gelding's stall. Searching,

he found the saddle blanket and slung it over the broad back. With a grunt, he lifted the heavy stock saddle from the top pole of the stall. Then he heard a scuffling behind him. Suspicion hit him, and he was spinning around.

One hand rigidly gripping a Colt, Dave Blanchard stepped from the office. His thin face was white and strained, the cheek bones like round, pushed-out knobs.

"Running?" His voice was hollow, and he attempted a sneer as he stood blocking the runway. "Owlhoots ain't so tough."

"Me?" Jeff wet dry lips. "I'm just riding out. Maybe I'm doing you a favor." But a question was turning over in his mind. Where was Ed Blanchard? Jeff's eyes flicked to the murky depths on the kid's right. Something was lumped there! It moved, and he saw the heavy-boned body of the older Blanchard shape itself along the light's edge. Ed's arm was bent, a gun in his hand.

"Drop that saddle," the voice grated harshly.

Slowly Jeff let the saddle creak down and stepped back. He shifted his gaze to the street, hoping to see Jim Banning.

"Not this time," Ed Blanchard jeered. "He's down the street . . . too far to help you."

"If I know Jim," Jeff said with a certainty he didn't feel, "he'll be comin' down here quick." But with a dismal realization he remembered how slow and tortuous the marshal moved.

The big man edged into the light, scowling darkly. "Come on, Dave," he snarled. "Make him draw."

Hands straight down, Jeff saw decision working along the straight line of Dave's mouth. Somehow the reckless challenge was draining from his face.

"Ed's prodding you, Dave," Jeff warned in a flat tone. "It's your hide, not his own, that he's risking."

Dave seemed to hesitate, and Jeff saw him swallow hard. There was a flickering doubt, almost revulsion, in the wide, fixed eyes. Yet he still gripped the gun stubbornly. Something flicked at the edge of Jeff's vision, a man running from across the street, as Ed Blanchard's voice shrilled: "Get him, Dave . . . now!"

In a blur of motion, Jeff saw Ed Blanchard wheeling. But his gun was swinging toward Dave, and Dave seemed frozen. Jeff's hand jerked, forking out the Colt. He whipped two shots along the rim of the muddy, confused shadows. His gun roared almost together with Ed Blanchard's—the flashes in the mealy light bright and stabbing. Lead whined against the stall partition, clapped off abruptly. Now Jeff heard a dragged-out grunt. He started to shoot again, but the broad frame was swaying. The gun hand dropped, and Ed Blanchard appeared to fold with a lazy, sprawling reluctance.

Spinning on his heels, Jeff saw Dave still standing. Boots planted wide, he stood rooted in a dull kind of haze. The pistol looked awkward and heavy.

"Put it up, kid," Jeff said wearily.

Dave let the gun drop loosely, as if Jeff's words were slow to sink in. His bulging eyes showed a puzzled astonishment.

"You . . . you went for him." Dave's grunt was choked. He shook his head. "You didn't draw on me."

Jeff heard the booming beat of somebody running on the street. He went past Dave and looked down, suddenly weary all through. Ed Blanchard was a huddled shape, unmoving.

Voices came to Jeff, high, excited. He heard Jim Banning call sharply: "Come out of there, Dave! Where's Jeff?"

Dave Blanchard was turning and muttering: "He didn't try for me. He got Ed."

"Good thing he did," Banning snapped. "You lucky damn' fool. I saw it, comin' across. Ed's been tryin' to frame you in a gunfight for a long time. I see it now. He figured you'd force Jeff Cole to draw. If Jeff missed, Ed was aimin' to get you. With you out of the way, Ed would get the ranch, and Jeff would be hanged for killing you . . . if you didn't finish the job." The marshal's voice lifted, calling urgently: "Jeff . . . you all right?"

As Jeff crossed to the knot of men, Dave glanced up at him sheepishly. "Cole . . . Jeff Cole," he said in sudden under-standing. "My God!"

Jeff didn't explain. He was looking at the gathering crowd. His head jerked up as he saw Delia standing to one side, hands clenched, pulled back against her. There was a girl there, too, big-eyed and dark. He elbowed a man aside and faced Delia. Her breath came drawn out.

"I came as fast as I could," she said. "Jim told me."

He was hungry and desperate for her, and he took a step. She looked up at him, and he held back. Her eyes dropped from his face to his shirt. Slowly her fingers reached up to the jagged tear of the pocket, and he felt the warm spread of her hand. His arms were sliding around her, and above the babble of the crowd he heard a girl's voice, like Delia's, calling frantically for Dave Blanchard.

Red River Stage

Lew Jenison had it figured out before he rode into Caddo Springs early that morning, for there wasn't much strength left in him. Despite a night's rest along the creek outside of town, he couldn't take another day's punishment in the saddle. The stage rolling in had decided him. He'd board it, rest while he traveled, and save time.

Some of his drive returned at the sight of the coach drawn up before the hotel. But when he dismounted, the numbed weariness was still there. His left arm felt stiff and sore. He tried not to favor it as he walked slowly inside.

A raw-boned, thick-shouldered man stood in the lobby. He turned, his stare blunt and stolid, when Lew stepped to the desk.

The southbound stage, the clerk informed Lew, would be leaving as soon as the passengers finished breakfast.

"I'll take a ticket to Red River Station," Lew told him.

"Red River Station?" The clerk hesitated. "Nobody ever gets off there."

"I'm going to. How much?"

"Sixteen dollars."

A sinking feeling deepened in Lew, but he said after a moment: "Hold me a place. I'll be right back."

"Yes, sir, mister. . . ."

"Early . . . Frank Early."

"Better hurry. Texas Jack's on the box today."

Lew went out, hating the thing he had to do. But he didn't have sixteen dollars. He led the gelding across the street to the livery barn and found the owner lounging in the runway entrance. He was a wizened man whose bargainer's eyes were already sizing up Lew's rangy dun.

"I want to sell my horse and saddle," Lew said.

"Happens I'm fixed up for both."

"Bet you're not for Morgan geldings," Lew said.

"You can't tell me anything about horses, mister." The sharp glance was busy again on the gelding.

"Then you know what he is. Make me an offer."

The runty man said nothing. Instead, he circled the dun and stopped at its head, his practiced fingers prying open the gelding's mouth. "I'll make you an offer," he said, dropping his hands. "Thirty dollars for the horse and saddle."

Lew felt a swift anger. "I didn't come in here to give 'em away."

"Take it or leave it. Any man who wants to sell his horse as bad as you do can't be choosey. For all I know, you could be Lew Jenison or Walt Flynn on the run."

"And you could get shot for loose talk," Lew reminded him tightly. "In the first place, that's no fair price."

"Just depends. If you don't think so, why don't you ask Ben Sitters?"

"Ben Sitters? Who's that?"

"U.S. Marshal. You'll find him at the hotel."

A cold sweat came over Lew. "You've got me over a barrel," he said. "The stage leaves in a minute. It's robbery, but I'll take it."

Moving back to the hotel, he saw the passengers filing out. The big man lingered out front, and something told Lew this was Sitters. Lew bought his ticket and boarded. He had scarcely seated himself by a window when he saw Sitters start toward the coach. A chilled dismay touched Lew as Sitters climbed in. Too late, Lew realized that in his hurry he'd overlooked the possibility of Sitters as a passenger. The next moment Lew relaxed. They were total strangers to each other.

Besides Lew, there were five passengers. There was, he learned as the morning wore on, a Miss Dant, also bound for Red River Station. Womack, a thin tubercular who was heading west, sat next to Lew. And rubbing elbows with Womack was young McNair, an Army lieutenant returning from furlough to his Texas post. Rambo, a newspaper correspondent from Chicago, was wedged between the girl and Sitters.

It was Rambo, chatting in his inquiring manner, who kept the desultory talk going above the grind of the six-horse coach.

"Mister Sitters, this is my first trip through Indian Territory. Do you expect any trouble with hostiles?"

"Some Kiowas busted off their reservation," the big man muttered, and left it there.

"No need for alarm, though," put in McNair, with a reassuring nod for Miss Dant. "A patrol works between Red River Station and Rock Gap." Blond and boyish, he looked very gallant in his cavalry jacket and yellow-striped blue breeches. A budding mustache topped his pink mouth.

Womack coughed into a silk handkerchief. "There's little we could do about it, anyway," he said, and took a morose drink from his canteen.

Lew didn't join in the conversation, and he noticed that Miss Dant paid little attention, except to glance at Sitters now and then. He decided she might be twenty, not a year more. She had an air of breeding about her. Her hair, worn long under her plumed hat, was so black it gave her well-formed face the ivory shading of a cameo. It was, he thought, a face that should have been amused and softly turned, but wasn't.

Sitters hunkered like an old bulldog watching his front yard gate. Whenever Lew looked at Sitters, the man's tenacious interest was always present. Lew tasted dust fuming up between the floorboards, and felt the July heat condensed in the confined space. He stared out the window, all tight inside, aware of the steady pounding within him.

Rambo's voice came again, suddenly loud in Lew's ears. "Mister Sitters, when I came through Kansas the papers were full of the Porter gang's last desperate raid at Pawnee Flats. It must have been quite a show . . . righteous citizens defending their little bank."

"What about it?" Sitters grumbled, annoyed.

Rambo's shaggy eyebrows lifted. "The story doesn't end there. Two men got away."

"Just who," Sitters asked softly, "would you have in mind?"

"None other than Walt Flynn and Lew Jenison. Where are they?"

"That's a good question," Sitters parried.

Lew, cold and tense, saw Miss Dant become quietly attentive.

"Flynn had a record," Rambo went on. "Jenison did not. He was a horse rancher, I believe"—he shook his head—"till the day he walked into the bank with the gang. In a way, it's puzzling."

"What's so puzzling about a bank robber? Nothing I can see."

"Maybe not. Anyway, the Eastern papers eat it up. And now we have a mystery. Are Flynn and Jenison alive? The posse found Jenison's dead horse. What do you think?"

"They're alive, all right," Sitters said firmly, his tone bragging.

Rambo looked pleased and waited expectantly for more. But Sitters did not elaborate, as if he thought he'd said too much already. Miss Dant eased back. The whole thing made Lew wonder what Sitters really knew.

The trail grew rougher, and talk tapered off. When the stage found smoother going, Miss Dant murmured to Rambo, her voice sounding rich and pleasant to Lew: "Do you intend to write an account of what you just told us?"

"Indeed, I do, miss, just as soon as I reach civilization again . . . say Fort Worth. And I'll wager you know something of general interest. There must have been considerable talk in Caldwell about the Porter gang." He paused, and his eyes appreciated her openly. "I suppose your father's in business there?"

She colored faintly, and Lew noted the level set of her small chin. She spoke distinctly, without apology. "My parents are dead. I sing in a music hall."

"Sorry, miss." Rambo covered up in haste. "No offense meant."

"Oh, that's all right. As for the Porter gang, I'm sure Mister Sitters, being a marshal and all, knows more about it than anybody." She turned to Sitters. If there were any guile in her smile, Lew couldn't find it.

Sitters squirmed and reddened. "Enough's been said," he replied.

Rambo grinned. Even Womack seemed to enjoy the byplay this once. McNair fixed his freshening interest in the girl, who showed just enough disappointment to make it convincing.

Lew speculated about her. Red River Station was no more than a jumping-off place for longhorn herds trailing north through the Indian Nations to railheads in Kansas. There was no dance hall at the river settlement, nothing for a pretty girl. In fact, she didn't even look gaudy enough to be an entertainer.

Toward early afternoon, with Fort Sill and a string of relay stations behind them, Lew sighted a rambling log house and corrals along the trail. This was Rock Gap, the last stop before Red River Station. A quick-eyed man, gripping his rifle, appeared in the doorway.

"Howdy, Augie," Texas Jack called. "Why are you all forted up?"

"The Kiowas are on the loose, or haven't you heard?"

"Yeah, we heard." Texas Jack's voice was scoffing. He called to his passengers: "Twenty minutes to eat and stretch!"

Like a jack-in-the-box, Lieutenant McNair hustled out to be the first to assist Miss Dant. A thin-shanked boy unhitched the horses.

Inside the low-roofed house, Lew looked around for Sitters. He was coming behind, and Lew sensed that Sitters had deliberately trailed him in. McNair and the girl entered. She chose a chair beside Sitters.

While a woman brought platters of greasy food, Augie told Texas Jack: "Britt's ranch was burned out yesterday. Why don't you wait up and go on early tomorrow with the patrol?"

"Wait?" Texas Jack drained his coffee cup. "There wouldn't be a stage line if we holed up every time the Injuns got wild." He rose presently, muttering—"Five minutes."— and took long restless strides from the smoky room.

Lew dallied over his coffee, watching the girl smile at Sitters. Then she stood up, and McNair sided her out.

Womack observed them, his eyes sick, bitter. "Youth and health," he said. "You can't beat it." He left with Rambo.

Lew went out, hearing the scrape of Sitters's chair as he passed through the door. There was yet time to kill before returning to the cramped coach, so he strolled to the pole corral. Several geldings, all bearing saddle marks, milled along the relay bunch.

His glance stopped on a saddle slung over a pole. Temptation took hold of him for a long moment; he let it grow. Then a scuffing sound rubbed at his senses. He turned.

"Nice saddle stock," Sitters said around his cigar.

Lew nodded.

"I don't figure Augie'd take to the notion of somebody helping himself."

"Wouldn't blame him."

Sitters scowled his exasperation. "You're mighty close-mouthed. What name are you using today?"

Lew felt the fear rise in him, but he looked Sitters in the eye. "Same as always . . . Frank Early."

"Where're you from?"

"Nebraska."

"Uhn-huh. As usual, it's from far off."

Texas Jack's restless—"Come on!"—rolled across the yard, and Lew strolled away, taking his time. He was seated when Sitters boarded the coach.

Womack was late. He puffed up, dangling his wet canteen. When McNair offered a supporting hand at the step, Womack rejected it scornfully. "I can handle myself."

Afternoon heat made everybody silent and dull. Now Lew saw broken hills black with mesquite and humped with rocks. Sometimes flat stretches of short-grassed prairie appeared. Mindful of his injured arm, he tipped his hat forward and pretended to doze.

The squeal of brakes aroused him. Texas Jack yelled in warning, and Lew, jerking up to look, saw stones blocking the trail. One shot slammed from the hillside. Texas Jack toppled from the driver's seat like a loose bundle.

Lew was moving through the door. He said—"Stay inside!"—and jumped down, hearing the racket of the frightened horses. Another report sounded as he ran forward. A lead horse screamed and thrashed down.

With a sense of shock, Lew bent over Texas Jack. One glance at the still shape was enough.

As Lew straightened, a whoop shrilled to his left among the mesquite-studded rock ledges. He rushed to the stage, to find Sitters and McNair piling out.

"Watch behind you!" McNair cried, and fired with the warning. There was a quick howl of pain.

Coming around, Lew saw coppery, half-naked shapes growing. He drove his shots at them, aware of McNair and Sitters working their handguns. Suddenly the brown figures broke and scrambled for cover.

"We can't stay here," Lew said. His eyes sought the uptrail slope, and fixed on rock rubble and boulders. "Let's get up there!"

McNair hesitated, glancing at Texas Jack.

"He's past help," Lew said.

Lew swung to the coach door. He reached for the girl, and she came willingly, light and tense in his arms. Womack lurched out behind her. He swayed weakly against the stage, his cartridge belt and pistol hanging ponderously around his slight frame. An arrow whispered and quivered in the coach paneling near his head. He jerked, and fired wildly.

Rambo came last. His black eyes were bright with fear, and he made an awkward picture gripping his pistol. Bleakly Lew guessed that he and Womack wouldn't be much help. They ran to the rocks through a scattering of bullets and arrows, Womack gasping at each step.

"The patrol," McNair said hopefully. "It'll be along."

"When?" Sitters growled. "Christmas?"

"Three, four o'clock, I figure." But when McNair eyed the sun, his shoulders sagged a little. "That means two hours' wait, at least."

Looking around, Lew saw how it was. They lay on a rocky rise, which offered fair protection as long as the Kiowas didn't get it in their heads to rush them. Below the stage, where the hills quit, he could see the flats and the pale scars of the road straggling across the brown prairie. It reminded him despairingly of Red River Station.

Thoroughly miserable himself, he glanced at and felt sorry for poor Womack, who already seemed finished. Womack breathed with difficulty. Sweat beaded his flushed face. His labored coughing was a pain to listen to. Lew looked away, realizing there was nothing he could do.

Rambo, he saw, had recovered from his fright. He kept staring about numbly, a vast disbelief etched in his face. Sitters had planted his hard vigilance on the Kiowas' positions— like a fox watching a rabbit hole, Lew thought. McNair sat quietly. Miss Dant made no complaint, and Lew found himself admiring her.

Something at the edge of the mesquite attracted him. Two warriors, crouched and swift, broke out like timber wolves. Screeching hate, they slanted straight for the coach. McNair and Lew fired almost together. One brave pitched and rolled, but the other raced on with drawn knife. It was Rambo, joining in, who knocked him down, just steps from Texas Jack's body.

"He wanted Jack's hair," Lew said.

Time dragged, and Lew wondered when the showdown would come. At intervals arrows slashed the rock. Miss Dant dabbed a tiny handkerchief to her cheeks. Womack mopped his punished face and lapsed into a siege of uncontrolled coughing. Moved, the girl patted his shoulder.

"If he just had some water," she said to no one in particular.

"Canteen's in the coach," Sitters growled.

A raw irritation burned in Lew. "You're a cheerful cuss, Sitters. That's what I like about you."

"I believe in facing the facts, that's all. You'd be smarter if you did."

Womack's coughing changed to a series of smothered gasps. Heat devils flickered in the glassy brilliance. Lew watched the sun edge slowly down its western course.

"About an hour yet." McNair was gauging the sky again.

Sitters's doubt followed like a dash of cold water. "What makes you so sure they still patrol this road?"

"It's a mail line. They have standing orders."

"Our luck's held this far," Rambo added, "except for Texas Jack."

"Luck's one item I don't depend on," Sitters said. "You never know when you'll be left high and dry." He hitched his thick-set shoulders. "Like this morning. A man in a mighty big hurry sold his horse in Caddo Springs. Would you say that was a mistake, Early, the end of his luck?"

"Who knows? Maybe that man's luckier than you think."

Everything had become quiet again. Womack's sudden coughing broke the lull. It hurt Lew to watch him fight it. The girl, who had removed her hat to shade Womack's face, patted him once more. Womack's feverish eyes mirrored gratitude.

Suddenly he wrenched to his knees. "Sorry, I can't stand it without water."

"You damned fool!" Sitters exploded. "Stay put!"

Womack swallowed visibly. A cough racked him. He

192

turned his bloodshot gaze around, and Sitters misread it.

"Expect us to get you water?"

A hot pride fired Womack's sick eyes. "Nobody's asking you, Marshal."

"Well, stay down. You'll draw fire."

There seemed to be an odd, furious strength working in Womack. He crawled several feet from Miss Dant, then whipped about. "Think I'd ask any man to risk his life for me?"

"I said stay down, you muddle-headed weakling."

Lew said: "Ease up on him, Sitters."

McNair's shout drew them all around. Womack was climbing uncertainly over the rock barrier.

The girl's shriek came as a tiny, piercing sound. "Don't let him go!" It was Lew that she looked to for help.

He scrambled up. But before he could grab, Womack had slipped away, running.

"Well," said Sitters, who hadn't budged, "it's his hide."

For that, Miss Dant gave him her killing contempt. McNair and Rambo watched helplessly.

The surprise of Womack's dash helped him at first, Lew saw, for not until he'd gone half a dozen steps did the Kiowas open up.

Lew yelled—"Cover him!"—and the four laid their fire on the ledges.

Womack was only a few feet from the stage when he fell. Miss Dant screamed and half rose, and Lew yanked her down hard. Womack seemed to want to lie there forever while he fought for wind. Lew heard himself shouting Womack on. Finally, in slow motion, Womack squirmed to his knees. He sank back, then heaved to his feet, reeling. He leaped wildly.

Lew's breathing stopped—and began again. It seemed impossible, but Womack was there, swaying, ducking inside the coach. He reared up with the canteen, clutched it high while he gulped. It was a long time before he put it down and looped the strap around his shoulder. For the moment he was sheltered, the stage between him and the ledges. The Kiowas weren't wasting precious lead or arrows on targets they couldn't see. They would wait, Lew realized darkly, until Womack started back.

The mocking stillness crowded against Lew. Miss Dant leaned forward, biting her lips, clenching her hands. Lew said: "Blast the ledges when he starts."

He felt every muscle in his body grow rigid as Womack stepped to the rear wheel and plunged into the open. Taunting screeches mixed with the weapons' roars. Womack took several strides, untouched. He came on in his dogged, weak-legged way that was neither run nor trot, grotesque and graceless. Lew had a surge of hope.

It was then it happened. One leg caved under. The impact of the bullet spun Womack. For an instant he hung in the air, his awkward, pitiful flight stopped. He sprawled, and Lew glimpsed his stricken face and heard the hair-raising whoops.

Somehow the sounds and the sight charged Lew with a cold rage. Then he was going fast over the guarding boulders, although he did not remember rising. It came to him that he was sprinting, and the curdling whoops were much clearer. A naked hackling swept up his spine.

Womack's agonized face took focus. Womack's voice grated hoarsely: "Get back! Get back!"

Taking a long breath, Lew lifted the wasted body, and was instantly shocked by the pain in his arm. A dim warning of sound came as he sprang up. He whirled toward it.

An Indian, his chest bloody, rushed howling from the stage, his knife high. There wasn't time to shoot. Lew dropped Womack and grappled for the knife. They collided and rolled, the warrior slashing. Lew clamped one hand on the wrist above the knife. He felt his shirt tear as the Kiowa grabbed with his free hand, but now Lew had the wrist in both hands. He twisted savagely. The knife clattered. He snapped it up and drove it downward with all his strength.

The thud sent a sickish reaction through him. It also stirred him to his feet, hefting Womack, running, tensed for the strike and rip of pain. But it never came. The smoky boulders were suddenly before him. He piled over and down, landing heavily. Rambo and McNair pulled Womack clear, and the girl became busy over him.

"Mister," Sitters said contemptuously, "you've got more luck than sense."

Rambo looked apologetic. "That Kiowa near Jack played 'possum. You were in the line of fire."

Lew could only shake his head, while he hacked for breath.

Miss Dant eyed him narrowly in alarm. "You're hurt. Let me look."

Lew drew back, moved by an unconscious wariness. He shook off her hand. "I just tore it. See about Womack."

She obeyed, although she was not quite sure. Sitters watched intently for several moments, before facing front again.

"They're coming now," said McNair, hollow-voiced.

Lew looked. Slim, arm-waving men, their bodies shining like wet copper, were running forward. Rambo fired hurriedly and missed.

"Let 'em come closer," Lew warned. "It's got to be a big killing."

Scorning concealment, the warriors closed in. Arrows snapped against rock. Lew could hear the pounding feet. Painted faces, streaked scarlet and white, glittered like masks.

When they were at point-blank range, he breathed—"All right . . . now."—and his gun roared.

For a moment the attack swept on, then all at once it melted. Ragged gaps came in the mass. Cries of frustration went up. But one brave, shrieking defiance, reached Miss Dant's boulder. Lew shot him in the chest and saw him topple backward. The whooping broke off, and Lew was surprised to find that he was holding her. She was trembling. He freed her and took a wary look.

It was just about finished. The handful of warriors was drifting away in sullen retreat, except when one wheeled to fire or spring an arrow. Presently they were beyond range, straggling around a hill. In a short time they were out of sight, traveling west on horseback.

It grew very still again. Only Sitters stood, gazing off toward the distant flats. Lew sat bowed, all the grind of the day hitting him at once. He loaded his pistol mechanically, and holstered it.

He wasn't prepared for Sitters's abrupt motion. There came a cruel, grasping pressure at the point of Lew's shoulder. He felt his shirt sleeve rip away, as he glanced up in dismayed astonishment. Sitters stood back, his pistol drawn. His other hand held a shred of shirt. Meaning exploded through Lew.

"Don't touch it," Sitters warned, when Lew made a motion toward his holster.

Lew glared. "What is this?"

"As if you don't know." Sitters slipped in and snaked out Lew's pistol. "You're Lew Jenison, heading for Red River to join Flynn."

"I tell you I'm Frank Early."

Lew was aware of faces turned in his direction, of the girl raising and asking: "How do you know he's Jenison? If he is, why didn't you arrest him in Caddo Springs?"

"Because I wasn't sure till he tried to hide that healed-over bullet wound. See for yourself." Sitters looked amused. "I picked up his trail on a tip in Caldwell. He hid out till he could travel, then started south. Now we can go to Red River and pick up Flynn at the Porter outfit's old headquarters, near there. I know where it is, too."

"You're all wrong," Lew protested, prepared for Miss Dant's loathing and contempt. But, raising his glance to her, he found an expression that both puzzled and warmed him.

At that moment McNair yelled, and Lew followed his pointing hand. Something moved on the flats. A line of dust was growing. Horsemen. It flashed over Lew that they'd been visible for several minutes.

He saw Miss Dant twist, her eyes raking Sitters. "You knew the patrol was coming. You saw them first, but you didn't accuse him till you were safe." She stepped as if to go between him and Lew.

Sweeping out his thick arm, Sitters batted her aside. As she sprawled beside Womack, a hot coil of fury looped through Lew, and he squared himself, fists knotted.

Sitters's gaze glittered. "Just wish you'd try it."

"Sitters, drop those guns."

It was the voice of Miss Dant, pitched high and yet determined. She had taken Womack's pistol, Lew saw, and she had Sitters covered from the side. Surprise froze Sitters for a second, but he still gripped the pistols.

"I mean it," she said.

Sitters drew in a deep breath. He hunched one shoulder to swing.

At once, Miss Dant fired. Flame darted as the barrel bucked, and Sitters dropped his guns as if they were hot coals. His face paled. He wasn't hit, Lew was aware, but she had shot close enough to convince him she meant business.

Sitters said: "You'll pay for this!" Shaking with anger, he glared at the others. "You going to stand there and let her interfere?"

Womack braced himself against a rock. "To hell with you, Marshal," he answered, and spat at Sitters's boots.

A change slid across Sitters's face. He turned to McNair. The lieutenant shifted his gaze to the girl and back. "That goes for me, too," he said, an enormous disgust in his speech, and centered his Dragoon pistol on Sitters.

Next, Sitters drove his inflexible will at Rambo, almost pleading. The ghost of a smile flicked about the correspondent's mouth—a tight, humorless smile. "I'd say you're outvoted by four, which makes it unanimous." He hefted his pistol up, and his next words were clipped. "Frank Early, or Lew Jenison, or whoever you are, I'm sure you know what to do now. You have almost all day."

Lew was moving even before Rambo finished, scooping up his own handgun and facing around. His stare went over the four of them, thanking them with his eyes. But as he stepped by them, the girl caught his arm.

"Take me with you."

"You?" he said, startled. "You can't go."

"I can't stay here." She refused to let go, and flung her meaning toward Sitters. "You know that. Please!"

Aware of time going fast, he checked the patrol—so close now he could see the fluttering guidon. It was Sitters's vindictive face that decided him as he whipped back, and the realization that he owed her something. He didn't like it, but he said: "Come on."

Sitters's angry shout followed them as they ran to the coach.

It took some moments to cut two horses free of the harness

tangle. Afterward, he boosted her up, and they rode east, away from the approaching column. Farther on they struck south.

There wasn't much of the day left when at last Lew halted. Not until now, with the broken bluffs of the river in sight, had he thought it safe to stop. "The station's not far," he told her. "You can make it from here. Thanks for helping me."

"You're not going in?"

"Not yet."

"But I can't, either," she protested, and it struck him how young and lonely and attractive she was. "Sitters must be close behind us, and nobody would hide me. He'd find me. I want to go with you."

"You must have people around here. Else why'd you come?"

"I do, but not at the station. Not close. Later I'll go to them."

"Look," he said, a roughness entering his voice. "I've got a chore to do, a dirty chore, nothing for you to see."

"But what could be so terrible? Tell me."

Time meant everything now, and he spoke fast, with a stored-up bitterness. "You heard Rambo say I'm a horse rancher. Well, that's how this started. Charlie Blue, a horse trader, asked me if I wanted some Morgans priced right. Naturally, I did. One day a man who called himself Walt Flynn came to my place and said he had the stock Charlie mentioned."

"You mean you didn't know he was an outlaw?"

"No, I was new to the district. He showed me his horses. They looked good, and we headed for Pawnee Flats to close the deal. Outside town, four men joined us, friends of Flynn's." Lew took a sharp breath, relieved that he could tell it to someone. "Flynn and I rode ahead. We started into the bank. Then it happened . . . the shooting. I ran for my horse, Flynn with me. It was that or get killed."

"Was he hurt?" she asked quietly.

"Don't know. About the time we reached the hills my horse went down, and I'd been hit. Flynn rode on. But I found Charlie Blue's ranch that night. In a few days Charlie brought in a bunch of Texas trade horses, and he had all the news. Flynn was holed up on Red River. Posses were looking for me. Just Flynn and myself got away. The rest were wiped out . . . Buck Porter's bunch . . . and Flynn was one of 'em. So I knew they'd used me to get inside the bank," he finished with a dull anger.

"And now?" she asked gravely.

"I'm going after Flynn," was Lew's savage reply. "He's the only man who can clear me. He'll talk if I have to kill him!

She became very hushed. Fear drained the color from her face.

"You still want to go?" he demanded, restless again.

"Yes. Maybe you'll need me."

They cut through a gap in the bluffs. Half a mile beyond, he made out the few buildings of Red River Station. As they rode up the river, something told him it was wrong to have a woman along. But a hurry came over him, and he put his mind to the rough footing.

"It's not far, is it?"

Something in her tone, a nervousness, drew his eyes. She sat straight and tense, watching ahead.

"We're close. Anyway, it's not your worry."

He was beginning to question Charlie Blue's directions when he spotted the weathered shack, all but hidden in the cottonwoods.

Lew dismounted and ordered: "You stay here. If I don't

come back, go to the station. Understand?"

She slipped down, giving him an uncertain nod, and he stalked ahead. Once he stopped and looked over his shoulder. She hadn't moved.

All was quiet in the tiny clearing around the shack, bathed in late afternoon shadows. He approached warily, his pistol drawn. At the shack's corner he halted, suddenly alert to a muffled stamping. A glance revealed the long shape of a horse in the timber. He advanced toward the door, feeling a tingling sensation.

"Walt! Look out!"

Lew wheeled and stared. The girl was shouting as she ran for the shack. For an instant he couldn't believe it. Then her betrayal lashed him like a whip. It broke his paralysis, and he bolted to the door and kicked it open. A dim bulk loomed, and he saw the gleam of metal. He dived low, into an ear-blasting roar.

He felt the man grunt in pain and go down as he lunged for the pistol. He kept expecting the violent struggle of a hard-muscled body, but Flynn seemed slow. Lew ripped the gun from his hand and flung it aside.

A wild elation crying through him, Lew grasped Flynn's shirt and shook him. "Flynn, you'll talk!" Flynn's head rolled, and Lew gritted savagely: "Y'hear me? Talk or I'll pistol-whip it out of you!"

Flynn groaned as Lew brought his pistol up. At that instant he discovered the crude bandages across the bloody chest. Flynn's face looked waxen. His breathing was broken.

Lew's rage was still a terrible, killing thing. Yet a queer stab of protest checked him. He caught himself slowly and reluctantly releasing Flynn to the floor. Flynn fell back, and Lew knew then that he couldn't do it.

Miss Dant came from the door and dropped on her knees

beside Flynn. She called his name, his first name. Flynn's eyes showed a glazed surprise.

"Vicky," he said, and his wondering voice seemed to come from a distance. "You came?"

"Yes, yes."

Lew could only stare at her, while a thickening disgust engulfed him.

"He's wounded," she said. In her anguish she turned to Lew. "Can't we do something?"

Lew's mind spun. Time was running out not just for Walt Flynn, but also for him. His voice sounded dead and flat. "We'll take him in."

He had his arms under Flynn's slack shoulders when he heard the sudden noise. It reached him dully at first, then grew quickly to the pounding of horses around the shack and men running and blocking the doorway. Ben Sitters's raw voice filled the room.

As Lew looked up, it came to him suddenly that he was beaten. His arms hung. He looked into the eye of Sitters's pistol; he made no protest when a man emptied his holster.

"Everybody outside." Sitters's face bore a triumphant grin. He glared at the girl and Flynn, instantly suspicious. "You, too, sister. Get up, Flynn!"

"This can wait," Lew protested. "Flynn's bad hurt."

"So what?"

"Shut up," Lew said, hearing the girl call. "Man, can't you see?"

Sitters stared hard. The shack got quiet. As Lew looked down, he heard her say softly: "Oh, Walt, you're in a bad way. At least you can help Lew Jenison . . . clear him of everything. Tell us. . . ."

Flynn's breathing was a tired, faint whisper. He said nothing.

"Speak for him, Walt," she persisted gently. "He's been good to me. He brought me here."

Lew saw Flynn's lips move—and then flatten.

"Then for me, Walt," she said. "And for yourself."

Flynn looked at her. He appeared to call on some last reserve of strength. His mouth stirred. "For you, Vicky, just you . . . because you came. We used Jenison for a front to get us inside the bank. We used a fake horse deal. That's the truth."

"He wasn't one of Porter's men?" she insisted.

"He never was."

Walt Flynn's fading voice seemed to hang in the room, until Sitters spoke in a let-down tone to Lew. "Well, your luck still holds. But what's she doing in this?"

The girl lifted her face to them. "I'm Vicky Flynn, Walt's sister. Isn't that enough?"

Purple dusk had fallen when Lew Jenison took the girl into the yard where the men were. Everything was over. When he saw her, so silent and stiff in the hazy light, a vast sympathy and gratefulness came over him.

"You're the only one Walt would have talked for, I see that now. You could have let it pass, though. Why didn't you?"

"For his peace," she said. "That was one reason. And for you. You couldn't beat him when you saw that he was hurt."

Ben Sitters came over. "Some things about this don't fit," he began, speaking to Vicky. "You claim you're Flynn's sister, but your name's Dant."

"Just a stage name," she replied. "When our folks died this spring, I came to Caldwell looking for Walt. I didn't want him traced through me. I never found him . . . till now."

Sitters mulled that over, then regarded her suspiciously. "Yet you knew he was hiding here?"

"No, I was following you, trying to find Walt before you did. To warn him."

"Following me?"

"Yes, Mister Sitters," she said steadily. "You had too many drinks one night in Caldwell. You talked in the saloon. A lot of people heard you." Her face softened. She took his arm impulsively. "But I don't hold anything against you. You did what you thought was right.

Sitters eyed her. For a moment his dark anger massed. Then gradually, by degrees, his face relaxed. With a grunt, he left them.

"You told me you had people around here," Lew said, "but I know you don't. That means I'll have to put you on the stage for somewhere."

She faced away, mute, staring off.

"Better yet," he said, "we'll go to Pawnee Flats . . . both of us."

That turned her toward him, as he'd hoped it might. "They tell me," she said slowly, a smile breaking through her gravity, "it's very pretty country."

About the Author

Fred Grove has written extensively in the broad field of Western fiction, from the Civil War and its postwar effect on the expanding West, to modern quarter horse racing in the Southwest. He has received the Western Writers of America Spur Award five times—for his novels COMANCHE CAPTIVES (1961) which also won the Oklahoma Writing Award at the University of Oklahoma and the Levi Strauss Golden Saddleman Award, THE GREAT HORSE RACE (1977), and MATCH RACE (1982), and for his short stories, "Comanche Woman" (1963) and "When the *Caballos* Came" (1968). His novel THE BUFFALO RUNNERS (1968) was chosen for a Western Heritage Award by the National Cowboy Hall of Fame, as was the short story, "Comanche Son" (1961).

He also received a Distinguished Service Award from Western New Mexico University for his regional fiction on the Apache frontier, including the novels PHANTOM WARRIOR (1981) and A FAR TRUMPET (1985). His recent historical novel, BITTER TRUMPET (1989), follows the bittersweet adventures of ex-Confederate Jesse Wilder training Juáristas in Mexico fighting the mercenaries of the Emperor Maximilian. TRAIL OF ROGUES (1993) and MAN ON A RED HORSE (1998) are sequels in this frontier saga.

For a number of years Mr. Grove worked on newspapers

in Oklahoma and Texas as a sportswriter, straight newsman, and editor. Two of his earlier novels, WARRIOR ROAD (1974) and DRUMS WITHOUT WARRIORS (1976), focus on the brutal Osage murders during the Roaring 'Twenties, a national scandal that brought in the FBI. Of Osage descent, the author grew up in Osage County, Oklahoma during the murders. It was while interviewing Oklahoma pioneers that he became interested in Western fiction. He now resides in Tucson, Arizona, with his wife, Lucile. His next **Five Star Western** will be THE YEARS OF FEAR.

Acknowledgments

"When the *Caballos* Came" first appeared in *Boy's Life* (10/68). Copyright © 1968 by the Boy Scouts of America. Copyright © renewed 1996 by Fred Grove. Copyright © 2001 by Fred Grove for restored material.

"The Marshal of Indian Rock" first appeared under the title "Town of No Return" in *Max Brand's Western Magazine* (9/53). Copyright © 1953 by Popular Publications, Inc. Copyright © renewed 1981 by Fred Grove. Copyright © 2001 by Fred Grove for restored material.

"Comanche Woman" by Fred Grove first appeared in THE PICK OF THE ROUNDUP (Avon, 1963) edited by Stephen Payne. Copyright © 1963 by the Western Writers of America. Copyright © renewed 1991 by Fred Grove. Copyright © 2001 by Fred Grove for restored material.

"Face of Danger" first appeared in *Ranch Romances* (2nd January Number: 1/13/56). Copyright © 1956 by Literary Enterprises, Inc. Copyright © renewed 1984 by Fred Grove. Copyright © 2001 by Fred Grove for restored material.

"Be Brave, My Son" first appeared in *Boy's Life* (5/65). Copyright © 1965 by the Boy Scouts of America. Copyright © renewed 1993 by Fred Grove. Copyright © 2001 by Fred Grove for restored material.

"The Town Killer" first appeared in *Texas Rangers* (9/56). Copyright © 1956 by Standard Magazines, Inc. Copyright ©